SAFE AT HOME!

SAFE AT HOME!

by Peggy King Anderson

1992
Atheneum
New York

Maxwell Macmillan Canada
Toronto

Maxwell Macmillan International Publishing Group
New York   Oxford   Singapore   Sydney

To my mom and dad,
who always made me feel safe at home

Atheneum
Macmillan Publishing Company
866 Third Avenue
New York, NY 10022

Maxwell Macmillan Canada, Inc.
1200 Eglinton Avenue East
Suite 200
Don Mills, Ontario M3C 3N1

Macmillan Publishing Company is part of the
Maxwell Communication Group of Companies.

First edition
Printed in the United States of America
Designed by Tania Garcia
1   2   3   4   5   6   7   8   9   10

Library of Congress Cataloging-in-Publication Data
Anderson, Peggy King.
Safe at home / by Peggy King Anderson. — 1st ed.
p.   cm.
Summary: As his mother tries to hide her drinking problem Tony
finds himself spending more time taking care of the house and his
little sister and less time playing baseball.
ISBN 0–689–31686–0
[1. Alcoholism—Fiction.   2. Family life—Fiction.   3. Baseball—
Fiction.]   I. Title.
PZ7.A54874Saf   1992
[Fic]—dc20
90-19133

CONTENTS

Contents

Christy and the Cocoa Puffs   **1**

Tony turned the corner onto his street, pedaling fast. He looked up, squinting his eyes against the afternoon sun. Almost home; just half a block to go. Boy, the house looked run-down. Now that the Bauers had painted, their own looked awful.

And the front drapes were closed. That was a bad sign. Mom always kept the drapes wide open, with a bowl of flowers on that little table, when she was okay.

The bike came down off the curb with a bump, and Tony almost lost his balance. He pedaled slowly into the driveway, then wheeled his bike around back and parked it in the shed.

He opened the back door and stood there for a

minute, listening. It was quiet. The muffled voices of an afternoon soap came from the family room. He sighed and went down the hall.

Christy was perched on the couch, her chin resting on her hand. She had on her Smurf pajamas. For six days straight now, she'd worn them to bed; they'd been a present for her fourth birthday last Tuesday. Here it was, 3:30 in the afternoon, and she still had them on. Her mouth was wide open as she stared at the screen. The TV voices were shouting as two women argued over some guy lying on a hospital bed with tubes coming out of his arm. Tony went over to the TV and snapped it off.

Christy looked up. "Tony! I was just gonna find out who killed Sondra's father."

"You shouldn't watch that junk, Christy. Why don't you watch 'Sesame Street' instead?"

"I already saw it this morning. And 'Electric Company' and 'Mister Rogers' too. Mr. Rogers got a new goldfish. His name is Bubbles."

"Where's Mom?" Tony asked, even though he already knew the answer.

"She's in bed," Christy said. "She doesn't feel good. But she came down this morning and made me breakfast. We had Cocoa Puffs."

"What did you have for lunch?"

"Peanut butter and jelly," Christy said. "I fixed it myself."

Tony walked back into the kitchen. Christy followed, her Smurf pajama feet slapping against the tile floor. Half a loaf of bread and an open peanut butter jar stood on the table. A second jar was tipped on its side, and strawberry jam dripped over the edge of the table onto the chair. Mom would have a fit if she saw this mess. He'd have to get it cleaned up after his paper route. "I'm hungry," Christy said.

"I'll fix you some soup in a minute. First I have to go upstairs and check on Mom."

Christy climbed onto the chair and scooped out a fingerful of peanut butter. "She told me she'll be better tomorrow, Tony. She said she'll take me to the zoo. She just wants to sleep today, and then she'll be all better."

"Sure," he said. He climbed the stairs, all of a sudden feeling very tired. Well, why shouldn't he be? He'd been racing around all day. The first day back after spring vacation, and all the teachers were loading them up with work already.

He forced himself to smile as he walked into his mother's bedroom. She was lying propped up on pillows. He couldn't see her face well. It was dark with the drapes pulled, and the room smelled stale, sour almost. He wrinkled his nose.

"Hi, honey," she said. She sounded sleepy. He went over and stood beside the bed. "How was school?" she asked.

"Okay. Can I get you anything?"

"Umm. Maybe you could pour me another glass of juice."

He looked at the glass container on the bedside table. His mom said she hated orange juice, but she always fixed herself a big pitcher of it when she was sick. This one must have been sitting there for a couple of hours. It didn't smell that great, and the ice had melted. "I'll fix some more," he said.

She answered quickly. "Oh no, this is fine, honey. I don't like it too cold. Here, I'll get it myself." She sat up and hurriedly poured a glass of the watery looking juice and drank it. She lay back down. "Now tell me about your day."

He stood there. Why was his stomach churning like this? She couldn't help it if she was sick. He searched his mind to think of something to tell her. He thought about the home run he'd hit during lunch break, but for some reason he didn't want to tell her about that.

"School pictures are next Monday," he said. "I need to bring money. Nine dollars and fifty cents for the economy pack. Do we have it?"

A slight frown crossed his mother's face, then faded away. "Of course we have it, Tony. You know I always make sure you have the things you need for school." She turned her face slightly. He couldn't see the expression on it now. "We got a check from Dad today. I'll cash it tomorrow, and set aside the nine-fifty for your pictures."

"When's he coming home?" Tony asked. "Did he send a letter with the money?"

"I don't know when he's coming home," his mother said sharply. "And yes of course he sent a letter. It's on the dresser. Go ahead and read it."

Tony picked it up. The sight of his father's hand-writing gave him a sudden catch in his throat. He stuck the letter in his pants pocket. "I'll read it later. I've got to go on my paper route."

His mother reached out for his hand. "I'm sorry, honey. I didn't mean to snap at you. . . ." Her voice faded off. "I'm just tired. I think I'll take a little nap. Be sure and tell me if the real estate office calls, though. I might have to show some houses tomorrow."

He nodded, pulling his hand away from hers.

"Oh, and Tony . . . can you fix some soup for you and Christy for dinner?"

"Sure," he said. He turned around and walked out of the room. When he got downstairs, Christy had the TV back on. She was curled up in his father's chair with her yellow blanket. She was sucking her thumb and watching a rerun of "Gilligan's Island."

"I'll fix you some soup and then I have to do my paper route," Tony said.

"Take me with you, Tony. I'm so bored of TV. I saw this one already."

Tony hesitated. If he took her, all the guys would tease him, like last week. But still, she had been shut up in the house all day. He felt the familiar struggle inside.

"Please, Tony?" she begged. "You can take the wagon and I can ride in the back and I'll put the rubber bands on the papers for you."

"I guess it will be okay. But you've got to get dressed in a hurry. I'm supposed to pick up my papers by four-twenty. Why didn't you get dressed this morning?" he said irritably. "You don't need Mom for that."

"I like my Smurf pajamas," she said. "And so

do the Nanakins." She padded up the stairs, dragging her blanket after her. Tony stood watching her for a minute. She was singing a little song as she went, but he couldn't make out the words.

So the Nanakins were back. Christy's pretend friends. He'd hoped she'd forgotten about them. All during spring vacation, she hadn't talked about them. Tony went out into the kitchen. Well, he had other things to worry about besides that. He had just twenty minutes to fix the soup and get over to the paper shack, or he'd get fined for being late again.

CHRISTY AND THE NANAKINS $\quad$ **2**

"I'm ready," Christy announced from the kitchen doorway.

Tony poured the chicken noodle soup into a plastic mug, filling it halfway. "Okay. We have to hurry. Here, you can eat your soup in the wagon on the way over—"

He stopped as he turned around and saw Christy. She was dressed in blue jeans and a pink sweater. That part was okay. But she had a purple fringed scarf wrapped around her neck, with the ends hanging down almost to her feet. She also had on her Cinderella crown from last Halloween, and she held a bouquet of purple plastic flowers.

He sighed. "Christy, do you have to wear that getup?"

"The Nanakins like it when I wear fancy things." She took the cup of soup from Tony, walked outside, and climbed into the wagon.

Tony shook his head. It was useless to argue with Christy about her imaginary friends. Besides, he'd be late if he didn't leave right now. He grabbed his newspaper bag and a handful of rubber bands and went outside. "The guys at the paper shack are going to give you a hard time," he said, picking up the handle of the wagon and starting down the driveway. "You'd better at least take off the crown."

Christy carefully set her bouquet of flowers in the corner of the wagon and drank the broth off her soup. "I don't care what those old boys say. The Nanakins like what I wear."

The wagon clanked as Tony pulled it around the corner. "The Nanakins are just pretend, Christy. You made them up."

"I did not," Christy said firmly. "They're my real friends and they stay with me all day while you're at school." She took the plastic spoon Tony had given her and spooned noodles into her mouth.

Tony sighed. Christy made up the Nanakins because she was lonesome. That wasn't hard to figure out. He felt suddenly angry at his mother for leaving her alone so much.

Don't be stupid, Tony said to himself. Mom can't help it if she's sick.

"Tony . . . Tony!" Christy's voice sounded urgent. "Aren't you going to the paper shack?"

Shoot! He'd walked right past the turnoff. He looked at his watch. If he didn't make it in three minutes he'd be docked. He turned the wagon around. "Hang on, Christy," he said. "I'm going to run."

She put her almost-empty soup mug in the corner and grinned up at him. "All right!" She clutched the sides of the wagon. Tony ran. The wagon made a terrible clattering noise on the sidewalk, and he heard his breath rasping in and out. He raced up the driveway of the paper shack at 4:20 on the dot.

Jay Watson and Craig Mondale were there already, shoving papers into their bags. Mr. Elliott, the shack manager, was watching with his arms folded. "You're cutting it close, Tony," he said. "Our customers want their papers on time." He looked disapprovingly at Christy, but didn't say anything more. Tony went over to his stack of papers and began to count them out.

Christy's eyes sparkled. "That was fun, Tony. The Nanakins love to go fast in the wagon."

Tony looked quickly over at Craig and Jay. Both boys were watching him. "How come you've got your little sister again?" Jay asked. "Your mom still sick?"

Tony nodded.

Jay elbowed Craig. "Get a load of her. Hey, Christy—Halloween isn't until October." He snickered. Christy ignored him.

Tony threw the papers into his bag and jerked the wagon back out to the sidewalk. "I told you they'd give you a hard time," he said to Christy irritably.

"I don't care." She carefully laid two noodles from the soup on her jeans knee.

"Well I do!" Tony said. "I have to go to school with these guys. What are you doing with those noodles?"

"The Nanakins like to have noodle-eating contests," Christy said. "One gets at each end and they chew toward the middle."

Tony sighed. "Of course. I should have known." He left Christy sitting in the wagon and started up the Morgan driveway, which seemed about a mile long. He looked around for the neighbor's dog.

He'd never seen the dog, but he'd been warned about him by the paperboy before him. He stuffed the paper in the box by the door and was just starting back when he heard barking. He looked up and saw the big black-and-white dog barreling toward him from the neighbor's yard.

He turned around and ran.

The dog ran too, barking louder. Everything was a blur as Tony tore down the driveway. He caught a glimpse of Christy, pink and blue and purple, climbing out of the wagon. He was too out of breath even to shout a warning.

Christy was marching toward him, he saw with disbelief, straight toward the black-and-white dog that was almost at his heels. Tony reached out for her, but she sidestepped him.

"You stop that barking right now," she said firmly. He spun around, trying to grab her, expecting any minute to feel the dog's teeth sink into his leg. But the dog was watching Christy with a confused look on his face. "Nice dog," she said. "Sit down and I'll pet you."

To Tony's amazement, the dog sat. Christy patted the dog's head and stroked his neck while Tony watched. But when Tony started to come up to him,

the dog growled. "He's afraid of you," Christy said.
"You be good now, doggie."

She walked away and climbed back into the
wagon. The dog sat watching her. Tony slowly
picked up the handle and pulled the wagon down
the sidewalk.

"How did you know he'd let you pet him?"
Tony asked grumpily. "He could have bitten you
instead."

"The Nanakins told me," Christy said.

The Letter $\qquad$ 3

French toast.

Tony smelled it as soon as he started down the stairs the next morning. The cinnamony smell was so wonderful it almost made him forget the letter from his dad. He still hadn't read it; what did it matter anyway?

His father wasn't coming home anytime soon; Tony could tell from what his mom had said last night. He shoved the letter farther into his back pocket and hurried down to the kitchen. His mom was taking two slices off the griddle. She looked up and smiled. "Morning, honey. Sit down and I'll put these on your plate."

He felt a little dizzy. He never could get quite used to this, how she would be so sick one day and seem fine the next. It was like being jerked back and forth between two different worlds.

"Mommy, can I have another piece too?" Christy was already at the table, a ring of sticky syrup around her mouth. She had on a plaid playsuit and her hair was brushed and clipped into two ponytails high on her head. She grinned at Tony. "Mommy's picking me up after preschool and we're gonna go out to lunch and then to the zoo, and I get to feed peanuts to the elephant."

Their mother plopped a piece of French toast down on Christy's plate. "Now don't be worried if I'm a few minutes late picking you up, Christy. I have to show two houses this morning, and then I need to stop at the bank and cash Daddy's check so we'll have money for lunch."

"And for my school pictures," Tony said.

His mother looked at him blankly. "School pictures?"

He felt that cold lump in his stomach. She'd forgotten again. "I told you yesterday. I need the money for next Monday. Nine dollars and fifty cents."

He felt almost desperate, wanting her to say, "Oh yes, honey, now I remember." But he could see from the look on her face that she didn't.

Maybe she had a vitamin deficiency or something. There had to be some reason why she forgot things so often, why she was sick so much.

She put the syrup and butter down beside his plate. "Go ahead and eat, Tony. You'll be late for school. I'll get money for your pictures. And don't look at me that way."

Well, how was he supposed to look at her? He wondered if other kids had moms like his—moms who couldn't remember what their own kids said to them twelve hours before.

He felt the familiar panic starting inside and forced himself to take a couple of deep breaths. Cool it, Tony. Don't make a big deal out of nothing. Everybody forgets things. Hey, she was sick when you told her. And she was sleepy. Yeah, that was it. She was half asleep. She didn't really hear you say it.

He felt calmer now. She had said she was tired. She'd taken a nap then. So it made sense.

He started to eat the French toast, cutting a bite, putting it in his mouth, chewing, swallowing. His mother kept talking in the background. "This may be my big break. The house I'm showing today is the old Hayden estate. And the man I'm showing it to is the vice-president of Western Bank and Savings. If he buys it I'll get a wonderful commission."

She put a glass of orange juice down in front of him. "If I make this sale, Tony, I'll buy you that baseball glove you've been wanting."

"What about me, Mommy? What about me?" Christy said. Mom planted a kiss on top of Christy's head. "And you, my munchkin, can have a Smurf Family playhouse." Christy squealed her delight.

Tony heard his voice coming out stiffly. "You don't have to get me the glove," he said. "I have almost enough money saved up already from my paper route. I can take care of myself."

He jumped up from the table. "I better get going. I don't want to be late." He gave his mom a quick hug, grabbed his book bag off the chair, and rushed out before she could say anything else.

But he saw her looking out the window at him as he wheeled his bike down the driveway, and she looked puzzled. Tony, you jerk, he said to himself. What's wrong with you? She tries to do something nice, and you act like a dope.

What *was* wrong with him? Things were good this morning. His mom was feeling better and Christy was taken care of for the day.

It was the letter, the letter that crinkled stiffly in his pocket as he pedaled down Jefferson Avenue. His stomach hurt, thinking about it. But he had to read it. Something inside him refused to give up hope. Maybe this letter would be different. He turned the corner, and saw the familiar swings of McFadden Neighborhood Park. He wheeled his bike over to the picnic table and parked it.

Despite what he'd said to his mom, he had an extra half hour before school, since there was an assembly today. He looked around. It was quiet this early in the morning. There was an old man by the duck pond, with a bag of bread. Two Canada geese honked loudly as they jostled for the biggest pieces. No one else was in sight.

Tony sat down on the picnic table and pulled the crumpled letter out of his pocket. He smoothed it out. The scribbled words seemed to blur into the page.

Dear Eileen and kids,

Hope all is well there. Tony, are you playing baseball? Hope you signed up for the team this time. I'm looking forward to seeing you in a game when I get home.

Christy, how's preschool? Send me some of your

paintings; I keep them in my briefcase to remind me of you.

I'm sorry it's taking longer than I thought to get this region going. We had a breakthrough last week. ITC, a big engineering firm, has contracted to use our services. Maybe it won't be too long now before I'll be able to come back home.

In the meantime take care of each other, and write me.

Eileen, hope you're feeling better.

> *Much love to all of you,*
> *Dad*

Tony crumpled the letter and shoved it back in his pocket. Why didn't his dad just make copies of the letter and drop one in the mail every week?

He wanted to believe his dad was coming back. It seemed impossible that just six months ago, he'd trusted his dad, played baseball with him, believed his dad cared.

But then he'd left, and everything had changed. The first couple of months, Tony had hoped he really was coming back, even though he'd had an uneasy feeling when his dad left so soon after that big fight with Mom.

Tony had written long letters, telling his dad

how he was doing on his pitching, how he was working on his fastball and his change-up. And each week a letter came. But they were always short, always talking about a breakthrough. Always excuses. Four months went by, and his dad didn't get home, even for a visit. The clincher had been when he didn't come home for Christmas. Even dads on the road traveling got home to spend Christmas with their families—if they wanted to.

And he remembered the look on Christy's face last Tuesday when Dad wasn't there for her birthday.

He got back on his bike and started for school.

Why did he keep hoping? He might as well face it—he and Christy and their mom were all that were left of the family now. And sometimes he felt like it was just him and Christy.

SAFE OR OUT?

4

"Hey, Tony—you ready to play?"

Craig stood impatiently by the cafeteria door, his catcher's mitt in hand.

Tony swallowed his last bite of hamburger and carried his empty tray over to the cafeteria window. "Sure," he said. He followed Craig outside. Several other sixth graders were tossing a ball back and forth on the grass.

"Don't get any ideas, Craig," Jay Watson said, as Tony and Craig walked out. "Tony's pitching for us today. You guys had him yesterday."

"C'mon, Jay. We had that fire drill and only got half an inning before the bell rang. And besides you guys are still two runs ahead from yesterday. We get him again today."

Tony grinned. He didn't really care who he pitched for, but it was kind of neat to have the guys fighting over him. Out here on the baseball field he could let go and just be himself. Out here he felt real.

Tony warmed up while Craig and Jay argued and finally chose teams. "All right," Craig said to Jay. "You get him today, but we're up to bat first."

Tony walked confidently to the pitcher's mound. He scuffed his foot contentedly across the hard-packed dirt. The ball felt solid in his fist as he wound up for the first pitch.

"Okay, Tony," Jay shouted. "Burn it in."

It was one of those days when everything went right. He hit his stride early in the inning and easily got the three outs within the first few minutes. He could feel the approval of his team. Today, right now, Tony was in control of his world.

His team was up then, but Tony didn't get to bat.

"That dumb Carson," Jay grumbled. "I counted on him to bat the others in, but he had to strike out."

"Time for one more inning," Craig hollered. "Let's go!"

Tony pitched an even better second inning. Nobody could touch his fastball. Craig got the only ball in play, and that was a pop fly that Tony caught easily, making the third out.

"Okay," Jay said. "You bat after me this time, Tony. Pete and I will get on base; then you'll get the chance to hit all three of us in."

Jay's cockiness made Tony want to laugh, but it turned out he was right. Pete and Jay both got on base, and Tony was up.

He stepped up to the plate, took a couple of quick practice swings, then settled down to wait for the pitch. When it came, it was a little high, but still inside the strike zone. Tony swung, and heard the satisfying crack as the bat hit the ball squarely. He took off for first.

They needed a home run now; there wouldn't be time for another inning, and the other team still had two runs left over from yesterday. He rounded first and headed for second, his feet slamming against the ground. The dust he kicked up made his nose itch, but he couldn't think about that. Concentrate on running. He had a good rhythm going, feet pounding the ground, arms keeping the beat. He heard cheering—Jay was home. Pete was almost there too, Tony saw as he raced toward third.

He heard the shouts then. "Tony! Hold up! Wait on third!"

Shoot. The outfielder must have snagged the ball on the first bounce. Well, it was too late to stop now. He rounded third and headed for home, the momentum carrying him, lifting him forward. I'll slide, he thought. I can make it.

Home plate was just ahead of him, coming up fast. Even though he couldn't see it, he knew the throw was on its way in. He could feel the energy as he raced the ball for the plate.

He saw Craig waiting, mitt outstretched, his eye on the incoming throw.

Tony hit the dirt, his body sliding toward the plate. He'd make it. He had to make it.

He saw the shadow, heard the smack of the ball hitting the mitt. A fraction of a second before his foot touched the plate, he felt Craig tag him out.

There was a huge cloud of dust, and he began to sneeze. "Safe! He's safe at home," Jay yelled.

"You're crazy!" Craig shouted. "He's out!"

The two boys stood over him, arguing. Tony stifled the tickling in his nose. "I'm out," he said flatly.

"You heard him," Craig said. "Told you he was out."

"I was closest! He was not."

"How could you tell? You had your eyes shut."

"Oh yeah?"

Tony pulled himself to his feet just as the bell rang, and started back to the classroom. Craig and Jay, still arguing, followed him, with the rest of the kids grumbling along behind. Jay caught up to him just as they got to the classroom door. "Well, hey—great game anyway, Tony. Are you staying after school tomorrow to try out for the school team?"

Tony shook his head. Jay looked surprised. "Why not? You're the best player in the sixth grade."

"I've got the paper route after school," Tony said shortly.

"So? I do too. We're not having practices right after school this year. Coach Egan has to do driver's ed over at the high school. Practice doesn't start until five-thirty."

Tony was silent. He was done with his paper route by 5:15 usually—but he'd have to come straight over to the field for practice. If he signed up. Then Christy would be alone again, all through dinnertime. But maybe . . . maybe . . .

"I don't know," Tony said. "I'll have to check

with my mom and see if it'll work out. I'll let you know tomorrow."

Jay grinned. "Great! If you're on our school team, we'll wipe out the other teams in the league."

They had a movie that afternoon in school, some documentary on hermit crabs, and all through it Tony's mind raced as he thought about what Jay had told him.

Last year, things had been so screwed up at home with his mom and dad arguing all the time that he hadn't said anything about trying out. Maybe this time he could play. His heart pounded with joy, just thinking about it. What would it be like to have that to look forward to—two hours every day, just to play baseball?

Spaghetti and Meatballs Forever

5

On his way home that afternoon, Tony went the long way around, so he could go by Thoreau School. The team was out practicing and he stopped to watch. Jay had said Thoreau was Sandburg's stiffest competition in the league.

The pitcher was trying to throw a fastball, but he was having trouble with it. The ball went wild every pitch. Tony's fingers itched, wanting to be the one down there on the mound. He'd worked hard on his fastball, and he had almost perfect control when he threw it.

Maybe this year things would work out for him to play for Sandburg. He'd talk to his mom and see how she reacted. If she didn't seem too upset, he'd do it. He turned onto Jefferson Avenue, feeling good.

Then he thought about Christy and her Nanakins, and the good feeling faded. If he played on the team, Christy would be alone more than ever. He mulled this over, wishing he didn't feel responsible for her all the time. He didn't realize until he wheeled his bike up into the driveway that he'd forgotten to practice wheelies on Jefferson Avenue.

The drapes were open and there was a vase of flowers on the table in front of the window. He opened the back door. Something smelled good. Spaghetti sauce—not the stuff in a jar that he usually heated up, but his mom's homemade spaghetti sauce. He couldn't even remember the last time she'd made it. He walked into the kitchen. His mom was standing at the stove, and the frying pan sizzled with the most wonderful smell in the world.

"Meatballs!" Tony said.

She smiled at him. "I figured you deserve a special meal every once in a while."

"I'm helping," Christy said. She was standing on a chair at the counter. She showed Tony the lopsided meaty blob in her hand. "Mine are crooked, but Mommy says they'll taste just as good."

She handed the meatball to their mom and wiped her hands on a huge apron tied around her middle. "And guess what, Tony? We really did go to the zoo and I fed the elephants and you'll never guess what else."

"What else you fed?" Tony said teasingly.

"No, silly—what else I *did*." She hurried on. "I got to *ride* an elephant too."

"You mean a pony, don't you?" Tony asked.

"No. An elephant. Really, truly! Right, Mommy?"

She nodded. "They're raising money for the elephant's new compound. Christy did get to ride the elephant."

"It was really bumpy, Tony, but I holded on good, and I didn't fall."

"Tony, go look on the dining room table," their mom said. "Christy and I made a special snack for you."

He looked. "Date nut bars. Super!" He took a handful and walked back into the kitchen. "How'd the house showing go?" This was one of the days when he felt safe asking. She seemed to be doing okay this afternoon.

"Great!" she said. "Mr. vice-president loved the house and has already called his wife to come see it. I'm taking them back tomorrow to see it together. I have a good feeling about this one, Tony. I think it's going to be my big break."

He grinned at her. "I hope so. Well, I'm going to grab a glass of milk and then I've got to get to my paper route."

"Okay, honey. Dinner should be ready by the time you get back."

Tony pedaled over to the paper shack, feeling the grin that kept popping out on his face. Things were looking up. This was the best he'd seen Mom for months. Maybe it had something to do with the weather. It was warmer this week.

That was probably it. She probably had some kind of sinus or arthritis kind of thing that got bad when the weather was lousy. Now with spring coming, she'd feel better. He'd make sure she took lots of vitamins and stuff, so she could build up her strength. By the time it started getting cold again, she'd be healthier and not get sick so often.

He pulled into the paper shack at 3:55. Mr. Elliott was just setting out the stacks of newspapers for each of the boys. He looked surprised as Tony parked his bike. "Good going, Tony. You're the first one here. The papers just arrived."

His newspaper count was okay, and Tony finished the whole route in forty-five minutes, with no signs of the neighbor's dog at Mr. Morgan's house.

He headed back home whistling. Christy was setting the table when he walked in. There was a red-and-white checkered tablecloth on it, and Mom was just setting a big drippy candle in the middle.

"C'mon, Mom," he said laughing. "Our dining room doesn't quite make it as Gino's Italian Restaurant."

"Then use your imagination," she said, smiling at him. She carried in the pot of sauce and meatballs and set it in the middle of the table with a flourish.

This was the mom he remembered, the fun-loving mom from when he was little—the one who flew kites and rolled down grassy hills with him. The mom who was hardly ever sick.

"Come on," Christy said. "Let's eat. I'm starving."

Mom carried in a pitcher of ice water and a plate of Italian bread and sat down. "All set," she said. "Tony, you say the blessing."

The phone rang in the kitchen, sounding loud and jangly. Tony jumped up. "I'll get it."

"Whoever it is, tell them to call back," Mom

said. "Tell them we are having a gourmet Italian feast, and it cannot wait."

Tony grinned as he ran for the phone. He picked up the receiver. "Hello?"

"Tony."

The deep voice was familiar. "Dad," Tony said.

The Phone Call   6

"How are you doing?" his dad asked.

"I'll get Mom," Tony said abruptly. His mom had left a dish towel on the table by the phone. The towel had a splotch of red sauce in the middle. He folded it, covering over the sticky sauce, and set the receiver down on it.

He walked into the dining room. "It's for you, Mom," he said.

"Tony!" She sounded annoyed. "I told you to . . ." Her voice trailed off as she looked at his face. She got up and went into the other room.

Tony sat down at the table. Christy had a ring of spaghetti sauce around her mouth. "I was so hungry I ate two meatballs already, but I said a blessing. I said the one Shannon taught me at preschool. 'Good food, good meat, good Lord, let's eat.'" She took another bite. "Try it, Tony. Mommy and me make good meatballs and spaghetti."

He picked up his fork and wound strands of spaghetti until he had a wad. He put it in his mouth, chewed, swallowed. He stuck his fork in a meatball, ate it whole, then quickly ate two more. Christy stopped eating to watch him, her eyes wide.

He ignored her. His ears strained to hear what was going on in the kitchen. Mom's voice sounded tense. He couldn't hear the words. A few minutes went by and she came to the dining room door. "Christy, Daddy wants to talk to you."

"Daddy!" She slid down from the dining room table and ran into the kitchen.

"Wait," their mother said, as she followed. "Let me wipe off your hands."

Tony ate three more meatballs. He could hear Christy as she squealed into the phone. "Guess what, Daddy! Mommy and me made spaghetti and I went to the zoo today, and I got to ride the elephant." There was a pause. Then Christy said, "When are you coming home? In a couple of weeks is Dad's Night at preschool and Jenny's daddy is coming and so is Todd's. Will you come too?"

There was another pause. Christy's voice was softer now. "Oh. Okay, Daddy. I will. Bye." He heard his mother again, her voice quiet. Christy came back into the room. She climbed up on her chair and looked at him. "Daddy doesn't know when he can come home. He can't come to Dad's Night." She took a bite of spaghetti, then put her fork on her plate and slid back off her chair. "I think I'm full of meatballs. I'm going upstairs. I have to tell my Nanakins something." She walked out of the room.

"Tony." His mother's voice sounded strained. "Your dad wants to talk to you." He walked into the kitchen and took the receiver from her. She left the room, looking upset.

His father's voice sounded too cheerful. "You got off the phone so fast, I didn't get to talk to you. How's it going? Are you taking good care of your mom?"

"Sure," Tony said. He swallowed down the flash of anger he felt. *You're* the one who's supposed to be taking care of her, he wanted to say. But of course he didn't.

"How's baseball going? Did you sign up for the school team?" his dad asked.

His own voice sounded stiff. "I can't. I have a

paper route after school." His voice kept going, like a tape recording that wouldn't stop. "I have to earn money for school stuff. If I didn't have a paper route, there wouldn't be enough money."

His dad sounded upset. "I send money every week for you and Christy. What does your mom do with it? Let me talk to her."

His mom was just walking back into the kitchen. Tony handed the phone to her silently. He walked out of the room and headed upstairs. But before he was out of earshot, he could hear his mother's angry voice, and this time the words were clear, even though they didn't make sense. "No, I do not drink up the money you send. What an asinine thing to say."

Tony raced the rest of the way up the stairs before he could hear any more. His heart was pounding. He felt sick to his stomach.

He lay down on his bed and took deep breaths, trying to calm down. But it didn't help. His stomach rolled and he felt perspiration break out on his forehead.

He went into the bathroom and threw up.

Dumb, Tony, real dumb. Shoveling in all that spaghetti and meatballs. His thoughts echoed in his mind as he lay on the bed and tried to talk his stomach into settling down. He moved his head to a cooler part of the pillow and lay still. It was quiet downstairs. The phone rang. Probably the real estate office calling for his mom. Well, at least it meant she wasn't talking to his father anymore.

Tony sighed. He shouldn't have said anything to his dad about the money. He knew that. Sometimes he didn't know why he did the stuff he did.

He sat up carefully. His stomach felt better now, just that dull aching. He went into the bathroom and washed his face. He might as well forget about baseball. Mom was upset now, so there was no sense even asking. He'd screwed up again, as usual.

He sat down at his desk and opened his math book. Lots of homework tonight. Think about that. Don't think about anything else.

There was the sound of footsteps on the stairs, and then a sharp knock at his door. His shoulders tightened. "C'mon in," he said.

His mother stood there, her arms folded, looking at him. Did she notice he was sick? He must look pretty bad.

She didn't seem to notice. "Your coach just called."

He tried to make sense out of what she was

saying. His coach? He'd expected her to say something about Dad, to bawl him out for what he'd said on the phone.

"The coach says he wants you to pitch for the school team. Some boy named Jay Watson told him you might be willing to play this season."

Part of the puzzle started to fall into place. Tony found his voice. "Jay. Oh, yeah. He's in my class. He asked me if I might be able to play on the team. I told him I'd check."

She looked furious. Was she that mad about him wanting to play baseball? Or was it the conversation with Dad? He hated it when he couldn't figure out what was going on. He looked away from her eyes, down to the math page in front of him:

$4A + 3A = 28$. *What does A equal?*

He took his pencil and figured it out. $7A = 28$. $A = 4$. Math was so easy. You looked at it and it made sense.

"Tony! Are you listening to me?"

He looked back up.

"I told the coach it's all right for you to play. He's sending a form home with you tomorrow for me to sign." He heard her words, but he also felt the tension in the room. Something was wrong. Something he didn't understand.

She turned as if to go, and then stopped. She looked at him and her eyes were accusing. "Your coach said he hopes I'm feeling better. He said he's heard I've not been well."

"I didn't tell him that," Tony said.

"Somebody did."

She folded her arms again. "Do I look sick to you?" Her voice was quiet, but Tony felt frightened.

"No," he said. "You look—fine."

"Well, I am fine," she said. "I've had an occasional bout with flu these last few months, but that does not mean I'm a sick person. There is *nothing* wrong with me. Do you understand?"

Tony nodded.

She walked out of the bedroom and shut the door. He sat there, stunned. His stomach gave another lurch and he sat very still and took deep breaths, waiting for the feeling to go away.

There was a small knock at the door. "Tony, it's me. I got something for you."

It was Christy. She didn't wait for him to answer, but pushed the door open and padded in. She had her Smurf pajamas on again, and a paper in her hand. She walked up to him solemnly and handed it to him. Her chin trembled just a little. "I heard you throwing up, so I made you a picture," she said. "See, that's the elephant I rode on today."

Tony looked at the gray blur in the middle of the page. "It's a great elephant, Christy. Thanks."

"The Nanakins helped me color it," she said. She turned around and padded out of the room.

UNCLE JEFF

7

Tony stood at the top of the stairs and listened. It was time for breakfast, but he didn't want to go down. He heard pots banging together over the sound of the dishwasher. He'd never seen his mom as mad as she'd been last night.

He went halfway down the stairs and listened again. More banging. Why was she so mad that the coach knew she'd been sick? He expected her to be upset about what he'd said to dad, or maybe even about him wanting to play baseball, but not this. He took a deep breath and went on down. He'd just have to cool it this morning. One thing for sure; there wouldn't be French toast today.

Christy was pouring raisins on a bowl of something when he walked into the kitchen. Yuck. It was oatmeal. His mother had her back to him, stirring the pan with the rest of the oatmeal on the stove. "Good morning, Tony," she said, but her voice was cool.

At least she wasn't sick again. If she had been, it would have been his fault for getting her so upset. But oatmeal. She knew he hated oatmeal.

Or did she? She hadn't remembered about his pictures, even after he'd told her. He really had no idea what his mother knew or didn't know anymore.

"I'll fix myself some toast," he said.

She didn't answer.

"Can you fix me a piece too, Tony?" Christy asked.

He put two slices of bread into the toaster and sat down. He poured himself a glass of juice, noticing his mom had a glass by the stove where she was working. He felt vaguely puzzled. How come she was drinking so much orange juice lately when she always said she didn't like it?

All of a sudden he thought of those last words his mom had said on the phone yesterday, just before he'd raced up the stairs. What had she meant?

No, this was dumb. Why was he thinking such

stupid things? All she was drinking was orange juice, for pete's sake.

"I put the nine-fifty for pictures in an envelope on the hall table," she said.

"I don't need it until Monday."

"It's there now. Just so you'll remember that I *do* take care of the things you need."

He sat there waiting. Now she'd give him heck for the stuff he'd said to Dad.

But she was looking at him, and her face seemed to soften for a moment. "Don't forget to bring the form home today from school so you can play baseball."

"Okay," he said. So. They weren't going to talk about Dad's phone call after all. He shouldn't be surprised. There were lots of things they didn't talk about.

"Tony," Christy said. "Can you come to my preschool for Dad's Night? Daddy can't come."

His mother turned around and he saw the annoyance on her face. "Don't be silly, Christy. Tony can't go for Dad's Night."

"Why not? Sarah's big brother is going. She said her daddy is dead, and so her brother is going."

His mother's voice shook with anger. "*Your* father is not dead. And Sarah's brother is much older than Tony."

Tony willed Christy to be quiet, to give his mom a chance to cool down. But Christy pushed stubbornly on. "Who can I take then? Everybody will have a daddy or an almost-daddy there except me."

Silence. His mother took a gulp of orange juice. Tony felt his pulse pounding in his ears.

"Would you like to take Uncle Jeff? I could call him." She sounded matter-of-fact.

Christy's face lit up. "Yes! I love Uncle Jeff, and we haven't seen him for so long, not since Easter."

His mother's lips tightened. She turned back to the stove. Christy never knew when to keep her mouth shut. Tony remembered last Easter, and Mom arguing with Uncle Jeff in the kitchen. Tony had been outside playing ball and when he came back in for a drink of water, Uncle Jeff stormed by him and out to the car with Aunt Karen following. He'd felt stunned. Uncle Jeff was Mom's baby brother. He'd never seen them mad at each other. Mom had gone to her room, so upset she stumbled going up the stairs.

That was the last time he'd seen Uncle Jeff. It was just one more of those things that happened at his house that nobody talked about.

"Tony," Christy said. "The toast popped up. Put lots of butter on mine." Tony buttered the toast and handed a slice to Christy.

She took it, tore it up into small pieces, and then spread the pieces neatly in a circle on her napkin.

"What—" Tony started to ask.

The Nanakins. Christy was putting breakfast out for the Nanakins. She looked at Tony. Her eyes crinkled, but she knew better than to say anything. Mom got angry when Christy talked about the Nanakins.

He jumped up from the table. "I've got to go," he said. "I'll see you after school." He gulped down the rest of his juice, and was out the door before his mom or Christy could say anything.

He felt better as he pedaled down the street on his bike. This afternoon he had baseball. Two hours of it. For the first time the realization hit him. He was really going to get to play! The tightness inside him seemed to melt away. Yeah, he thought. Baseball. Throwing the perfect pitch, and the slam of the ball against the bat when he hit a home run.

He turned onto Jefferson Avenue feeling better every minute. He popped a wheelie on the curb strip and smiled when he came down without a wobble.

SOMETHING ISN'T RIGHT   8

It was an okay day at school. Not much work, because of parent conferences the next week. He watched two science documentaries. During study time he read almost four chapters of *Baseball Heroes of the Sixties.*

After school was over he headed for the bike rack. Jay was going by on his way to the bus stop. "Don't forget, Tony. First practice tonight at five-thirty."

Tony nodded. "I'll be there." He thought about his mom on the way home from school. He wasn't going to let her get him down, not this time. Not when he finally had a chance to do what he loved best in the whole world.

She'd had moods before. Maybe not quite this

way, but she'd get over it. He'd check on Christy, do his route, and then head back for practice. At least in baseball, he knew what to expect.

The front drapes were pulled, and the house looked dark when Tony came in. No one was home. He found a note taped to the refrigerator.

Christy and I at mall. Home about 5:00.
Don't forget form from coach.

He grinned. This was great! He had the house to himself. He turned on the radio to a country station, his favorite, though it drove his mom bananas. He had to admit the words of the songs were dumb, but the rhythms were great. He whistled around the kitchen, the radio full blast, while he hunted for a snack. The leftover date nut bars were on the counter, but just the thought of them made his stomach turn. He'd better get a sandwich, so he'd have energy for practice.

He made two toasted cheese sandwiches and ate them while reading the sports section from the morning paper. He took a look at the clock and headed for the paper shack.

His route went fast again today and he arrived at McFadden Park fifteen minutes early for practice.

He didn't know if he was supposed to bring anything. He had his old glove, but it was in really
bad shape. Maybe he could collect from his route
a few days early and get his new one by next Monday.

He saw Jay heading toward him from the other
side of the park. "Hey, Tony! You made it!" He
grinned. "We'll wipe Thoreau off the map, with
you pitching for us. They think they're hotshots,
after winning the championship last year, but we'll
change that. C'mon, let's warm up while we wait
for Coach."

Coach Egan showed up a few minutes later.
Tony saw him standing there watching. He pitched
one to Jay as hard and as fast as he could. It went
right over the plate, and Tony couldn't help but feel
pleased. Coach Egan didn't seem impressed. "Hey,
Jay. You and Tony get over here and put out the
bases. Then you can start running laps."

Jay sighed. "C'mon, we'd better do what he
says."

Several of the other boys had drifted onto the
field now and were running laps. When Tony joined
them, he heard plenty of grumbling. "I hate running
laps," Chris wheezed. "I'll be so wiped out, I won't
be able to run the bases."

Tony didn't mind the running. It felt good to push his body a little.

But by the end of the practice, he was wiped too. Coach Egan was tough, and he hadn't oohed and aahed over his pitching. Tony was disappointed. When he sat on the bench and bent over to change back to his street shoes, every muscle in his body complained.

He'd just picked up his jacket and was walking off the field when Coach called him over. His voice was gruff, but his words were honey to Tony's ears. "Keep up that pitching, and you'll be starting for us on the twenty-fifth."

He felt like he'd explode with joy. When Coach walked away, Tony looked down at his feet to see if he was still on the ground. Jay walked toward him, grumbling. "Boy, am I tired. And just wait; this was the first night. He keeps adding laps every practice. Tomorrow he'll give us push-ups too."

"Hey, you kept telling me how much fun this was going to be," Tony said.

"I wanted you to sign up. Besides, the games are fun. It's just the practices that are a drag sometimes. Coach works us too hard."

Tony didn't mind the hard work. Especially not now, when he knew he had a chance of being starting pitcher. Besides, on the baseball field, he knew what to expect. He liked that.

The next two weeks went by fast. Tony could feel his body getting stronger every day, feel himself getting more control over his pitching. You put in a certain amount of effort on the field, you got it back in performance.

If only the rest of his life were like that.

Ever since that phone call from his dad, something was wrong at home—more wrong than it had been before. But he couldn't put his finger on what it was. Every so often, he thought about the conversation he'd overheard, the comment about the drinking, but he'd push it quickly out of his mind. It didn't make any sense. Probably he'd just misunderstood.

His mom wasn't sick anymore. She was up every day. She was catching up on stuff she'd let go for months. Tony had underwear that fit him for the first time since his dad had left, and new sweat socks. She was doing the laundry. He had clean clothes in his drawer every night.

But something was upsetting her and Tony could feel it. She was tense, irritable, jumping on him for nothing at all. It was scary, like there was a sharp piece of glass inside her that could break at any minute. He almost liked it better when she was sick and stayed in bed. At least then he didn't feel this constant tension.

There hadn't been any more letters or calls from his dad either. Up until lately, a letter had arrived every week, usually on Monday, never later than Tuesday. Not that Tony cared. But it was still weird.

On Wednesday of the second week, he asked his mom about it. "Did we get a letter from Dad this week? I—we have to get fifteen dollars in for the team registration."

His mother's face got all cold and hard. It happened a lot lately, but Tony still felt a knot in his stomach. "I've already mailed the registration check to the coach. I told you I can take care of the things you need. And no, we did not get a letter from your father."

Tony stood there, frozen to the spot by his mother's challenging look. Where did you get the money for the registration? he wanted to ask. And for the underwear and socks? But the look on his mother's face kept the words locked inside his throat. She turned away and walked abruptly out onto the deck. Conversation over.

Something was definitely wrong. His first game

was coming up this Friday, but he didn't even feel like telling her about it, not with the way she jumped on him about everything lately.

At least Christy seemed okay these last couple of weeks. She was getting to preschool all the time now—not missing like she had before when Mom was sick and it was her day to do car pool. And she and Mom did lots of stuff together in the afternoon, so Christy didn't sit around watching TV all the time. She didn't talk so much about the Nanakins anymore either.

"Guess what, Tony?" she said the following Monday. "We're not having Dad's Night at pre-school this week. Josie and Kara got chicken pox and now today Jeremy and Michael didn't come, and Miss Julie says they probably have chicken pox too. So we're not going to have Dad's Night until three more weeks. Maybe Daddy will be home. Then Uncle Jeff and Daddy can *both* go and it will be like I have two daddies. So *ha* on Melanie!"

Tony looked at her. "Why ha on Melanie?" he asked.

Christy crossed her arms. "She keeps saying I don't have a Daddy anymore. But it's okay. I fixed her. I hit her with the sand shovel Friday and she didn't say it at all today."

TAKING OUT THE TRASH

On Friday when Tony came down for breakfast, Mom kissed him on the cheek and handed him a plate of scrambled eggs. He looked at her, surprised. She seemed okay—not tense and upset like she'd been this last couple of weeks. "We play Thoreau tonight," he said impulsively. "I'm the starting pitcher. Want to come?"

"Tony, that's wonderful! But why didn't you tell me before?"

He shrugged his shoulders, not sure what to say. She didn't seem mad though. "I think I can come. The house deal is supposed to clear this afternoon. We're just waiting for the appraiser's report and that should be in today."

So that was why she seemed calmer. He took a piece of toast and buttered it. He felt a sense of relief. Maybe that was why she'd been so uptight these past few weeks. Business stuff, about the house she was selling to that bank vice-president. She'd said it was a really big deal. Sure, that was it. Things would be okay now.

"Do you think you might get a chance to wash my uniform?" he asked hesitantly. "I need it for the game."

"Of course, honey. Is it in your room?"

He nodded.

She handed another plate of eggs to Christy, who was putting a huge blob of strawberry jam on her toast. "Not so much, Christy."

Christy didn't say it, because Mom would get mad, but Tony knew what she was thinking. She'd already told him the Nanakins loved strawberry jam. He rolled his eyes and she grinned at him.

"Tony," his mom said. "If the house deal clears today, Christy and I will take you out for dinner afterward to celebrate. We'll go to Happy Jack's."

"Yea!" Christy said. "I'll get a double cheese-burger."

Tony pulled her ponytail. "You can't eat a double cheeseburger. You can't even finish a single one."

"Yes I can," Christy said. "The Nanakins—"
She stopped and looked guilty.

Mom looked at Christy. Her lips tightened. Tony jumped up from the table. "Well, I'd better get going. Jay's coming early so we can practice before school."

His mom turned and gave him a hug. "Okay, honey. Empty that wastebasket on your way out, would you? It's really full. Leave it by the gate and I'll get it later."

"Sure," Tony said. He slung his book bag over his shoulder and grabbed the wastebasket. It was piled high, but a lot of it was papers, so it wasn't heavy. "See you, Mom. Bye, Christy." He went out, pushing the back door closed with his foot. He maneuvered his way past his bike, which he'd left lying out last night. The trash can was leaning against a brick, and when he pulled the lid off, it tipped, spilling garbage and papers all over.

Shoot! He wanted to get to school early so he'd have time to practice his curve. He leaned his book bag against the tree and started gingerly shoving stuff back in the can.

What a mess. He got the shovel from the shed. That was better. He had most of it back in when his shovel clinked against glass. He stopped and bent over to see what he'd hit. A liquor bottle. Two of them. Vodka bottles.

What were they doing there? Maybe someone walking by in the alley had tossed them in. Or maybe the real estate agents had a little drink at their meetings or something. Yeah, that was probably it. His mouth felt dry as he shoved the last few handfuls of paper into the can. He dumped the wastebasket hastily. A torn envelope fluttered to the ground. He was tempted to leave it and take off; it was getting late. But his mom was a nut for neatness; she'd griped before about papers lying around by the trash can. He bent over and picked it up. Familiar handwriting was scrawled across the envelope in his hand—his father's handwriting.

But his mother said she hadn't heard from him. His hand shook a little as he stared at the envelope. Cut it out, Tony, he said to himself. You're doing it again, getting paranoid over every little thing that happens. It's probably an old envelope that got stuck on the bottom.

He turned it over. It was postmarked last Saturday. He fished around in the papers, hunting for the letter that might have been in it. He found two more torn envelopes with his dad's handwriting, both postmarked within the last two weeks. He hunted but he couldn't find the letters.

He shoved the lid back down on the trash. Why had she lied to him?

He grabbed his bike and took off, pushing the gate shut as he tore out. His hands felt cold and he had to keep swallowing down the taste of breakfast.

So she was mad at Dad and didn't want to let me know she got a letter from him. So what?

What about the vodka bottles? He clenched his jaw. *A real estate meeting, you dope, that's what they're from.* He hunched over his handlebars and sped down Jefferson Avenue. He was so tired of confusion, of not being able to figure out what was going on.

He skimmed along the curb and jumped the bike out into the street. *I don't care,* he decided. *I'm not going to think about it. Tonight is my first game. This isn't going to ruin it.*

Jay waved at him from the corner. "Hey, Tony. We've still got twenty minutes before the bell to practice. I'll race you!"

Tony caught up with him in front of the school. "How's it going?" Jay said. Tony looked at Jay's open grin, with the one chipped tooth in front from a ball that had taken a bad hop.

"Great," Tony said.

But he had to look down when he said it.

THE OTHER BOTTLE 10

Things started out all wrong. Tony blew three pitches in a row. The first two went in the dirt, while the next one was so high Jay had to jump to catch it.

"What's wrong with you this morning, Tony?" Jay sounded annoyed. "If you can't do better than that, we haven't got a chance against Thoreau tonight."

Concentrate, Tony told himself. The game. That's what's important.

But he couldn't stop thinking about the envelopes in the trash. There's got to be a reason for it, Tony told himself.

But was it really such a big deal? His mom knew

he was mad at his dad. She probably figured the letters would make it worse. He gripped the ball and got ready to throw a curve. Anyway, she was lots better this morning. So why was he getting himself so worked up? She was going to come to his game, was even going to take him out to dinner afterward. Like she said—there was nothing wrong.

"Better," Jay said.

"Huh?"

"You're pitching better now. At least you're throwing strikes. Come on—burn one in. Gimme some heat!"

He did.

By the time school was out, Tony felt okay. Focus on the game, he reminded himself, as he pedaled into the driveway after school. He just had enough time to grab a snack, do his route, and get over to the field for a pregame warm-up.

His mom was on the phone when he came in, holding a sheaf of papers in her hand. "What do you mean, structural damage?" she was saying. "That Hayden estate is in excellent shape. We had our own appraiser check it before we put it on the market." The tightness was back in her voice, worse than before. Tony stopped, frozen to the spot. There was a long silence.

"Damn!" his mother said.

He felt stunned. He'd never heard her swear before.

Christy came pounding down the stairs, two rainbow-colored ribbons in her hand. "Mommy. I'm almost ready. Can you do my ponytails?"

"Quiet, Christy," their mother said sharply. "Can't you see I'm on the phone?"

Christy stood still on the stairs. Then she stuck her chin out, and walked the rest of the way down. "Tony," she said. "Will you do my ponytails? Me and Mommy are getting ready to go to your game."

He'd done her hair lots of times before, the times when his mom had been sick, but he'd never been good at it.

"Okay, but I don't have much time, Christy. I have to get my route done, and get over for the game myself." Clumsily he brushed her hair into two ponytails, clipped them, and tied on the ribbons. They were lopsided but they'd have to do.

"Damn!" his mother said again, and this time she threw the papers down onto the floor. Tony stared as they fluttered in all directions.

There was no time. He had to get over to the paper shack now. "Come on, Christy," Tony said. "You can go on my route with me." He was surprised at how normal his voice sounded.

Christy stood there for a moment, looking like she was going to argue. Then she followed Tony outside to the wagon. She climbed in and settled herself. "We'll have to hurry," she said. "Mommy and me are going over early for your game."

Tony didn't say anything as he pulled the wagon over to the shack. For once, Christy was quiet too.

He picked up the papers, ignoring the smirks from the other boys as they looked at Christy sitting in the back of the wagon. Jay and Craig weren't there—Tony guessed they'd come in already so they could get to the field early. He threw the papers and his bag of rubber bands into the back of the wagon. Christy started rolling papers and rubber-banding them.

Just after they'd passed the Morgan house, Tony remembered his uniform. His stomach felt cold as ice. "Christy . . . you don't know if Mom washed my uniform, do you?"

Christy nodded. "She washed it this morning, and she dried it, and she put it on your bed, and she even put a note on it that says, Good Luck." She handed him a rubber-banded paper. "What happened, Tony? How come Mommy's so mad?"

Tony shrugged. "I don't know. Was she mad all day?"

Christy shook her head. "We had a fun day. I got to call Uncle Jeff all by myself. Mommy wrote the numbers for me and Uncle Jeff said he'd come to Dad's Night that got changed because of chicken pox. He talked to Mommy too and she sounded happy. I don't know what happened. I think it was something from the mail. The Nanakins and me have been thinking about it."

Tony's throat felt tight. "I think it's just something about the real estate deal, Christy. Don't worry about it. It will be okay tomorrow."

"But, Tony. We were going to go to your game, and now what if Mommy won't go? Can I go anyway? I'll be really good and sit still."

Tony turned the wagon around. Just four more houses and they were done. "Maybe Mom will be feeling okay when we get home, Christy. Let's wait and see."

But when they got home, she was nowhere in sight. The real estate papers were still scattered all over the kitchen floor, and an empty can of orange juice sat on the counter, with splashes of juice beside it. The cupboard door was open.

The knot in Tony's stomach tightened. His mom never left a mess. She was neat, even when she wasn't feeling good. Christy didn't say anything. She climbed the stairs and went to Mom's bedroom. "Mommy, it's time for us to go to Tony's game now." Tony heard his sister's voice, loud in the quiet house.

He couldn't hear the response, but when Christy came down, the look on her face told him everything. "She's sick," Christy said. "Please let me go with you, Tony. I don't want to stay here. I don't want to!" Christy's voice sounded almost desperate and Tony felt a moment of panic. But he couldn't take her, not without a grown-up. Not for the first game.

His voice when he spoke was calm. "You can go to the game next week, Christy. I'll get Jay's mom to take you. It's too late now. Here, let's check the TV schedule."

He grabbed the paper and turned to the program section. "Hey, Christy! *Lady and The Tramp* is on."

She followed Tony into the family room and

curled up in the big chair with her blanket. He felt awful leaving her, but he didn't know what else to do.

"I'll bring you back a treat, Christy. I'll stop at McDonald's after the game and get you some french fries."

"A sundae," Christy said, looking up at him with unhappy eyes. "Me and the Nanakins want a hot fudge sundae."

Tony nodded, then ran up the stairs. He was late, really late. He should have left for the game already. Christy was right though; the uniform was pressed and ready on his bed. There was a note on top of it:

Tony, here's your uniform. Now do you believe I'm taking good care of you?   *Love, Mom*

There was a smiley face at the bottom and in big letters: GOOD LUCK TONIGHT!

Tony crumpled up the note and shoved it into the wastebasket. He changed as fast as he could, and started back down the stairs on a run. He hesitated, then went back up and poked his head into his mom's bedroom.

"Mom?" he said questioningly. She didn't answer. She must be asleep, he thought. "I'm leaving now," he said, just in case she could hear him. "Christy's okay. She's watching TV. I'll be back about nine."

There was no response from his mother. He strained his eyes to see into the dimness of the room. He could make out the pitcher of orange juice beside the bed, and beside the juice, a familiar bottle.

It was a vodka bottle, identical to the two he'd found in the trash yesterday.

But this one was half-full.

THE ROLLER COASTER   **11**

As he rode over to the field, his mind raced. This dumb memory kept pushing to the top. When he'd been five, his dad had taken him on the roller coaster at Seattle Center. He remembered sitting on the roller coaster, hanging on to the bar with both hands, his dad's arm tight around him, as they slowly cranked their way to the top of the first rise. He remembered the feeling in the pit of his stomach as they came closer and closer to the top, and he realized that they were going to go hurtling down on the other side.

He'd wanted to get off. He'd begged Dad to make the roller coaster stop, but there was nothing his father could do.

That was the way he felt now. He was on the

top of the roller coaster, and any minute he was going to go plunging down—and there was nothing he could do to get off.

His mom had been drinking. It didn't make any sense. She used to have a drink or two, a long time ago. She and his dad both did, but then they'd quit. He didn't know why. And he hadn't seen his mom with a drink for a long time, until today.

Except for that orange juice she drank all the time lately.

Cut it out, he said to himself. You're imagining things again. She's sick, just like the other times. She'll be okay. Think about the game. Think about your pitching. Think about that curve you've been working on.

He turned the corner, pedaling faster. He was ten minutes late for the warm-up already. He hated leaving Christy. Maybe he should have brought her. But what would he have done with her? He didn't know the other moms well enough yet to ask if she could sit with them.

Why wasn't his dad in town? Then he wouldn't have to figure all this stuff out himself. He felt suddenly furious at his dad.

When he got to the park Jay came running up to him. "You're late, and Coach is having a fit. He was just telling Johnny he might have to start." Jay grabbed the handlebars of Tony's bike. "I'll chain this up. Go ahead—you have to get warmed up."

Tony ran over to where the coach was talking to Johnny Scanelli. Johnny's face lit up when he saw Tony. "Hey, Coach. It's okay. Here he is now."

The coach whirled around. "Where the heck have you been?"

Tony didn't know what to say. He just stood there. Coach was watching him intently. "You've got to be on time for the games, Tony, or I can't use you as pitcher. Get over there now and warm up."

Tony took a deep breath. Get it together, he said to himself. He took his position on the mound and tried to concentrate on the ball, to will the energy churning inside him to go through his arms and send the ball straight to the plate.

The ball slammed into Jay's mitt. Tony could see Jay grinning at him through his catcher's mask. "Right on target, Tone. Keep that up and we've got it made." He threw the ball back.

Tony bit his lip and wound up. He threw another fastball, nice and low—but not too low. He could see the Thoreau pitcher out of the corner of his eye.

Jay walked out to the mound and handed Tony the ball. "Good going," he said. "Look at that guy's face." He nodded toward the Thoreau dugout. "You've got him scared already."

Tony looked, and grinned. Jay was right. He was going to be okay. He was where he belonged, on the ball field. There were rules here, and order. He knew what to expect.

The game started. Tony's first pitch whistled across the plate. The second one seemed to almost stop as it floated over. Expecting another fastball, the batter swung too soon and missed. Tony let out his breath. Everything was going to be okay.

And it was. The first three batters struck out and then Sandburg was up to bat. Jay got a solid hit while Craig was on second, and both of them scored runs. At the end of the first inning, Tony's team was leading 2-0, and the parents in Sandburg's bleachers went wild. Tony tried not to think about how much Christy would have enjoyed this.

In the second inning, things got tighter. Two of Thoreau's batters got on base, and fifteen minutes into the inning, they only had two outs. Only Craig's top-notch fielding kept the runner on second from scoring when the next Thoreau guy at bat clouted a solid hit down the third-base line.

But the bases were loaded now and Tony was starting to sweat. He had to get that third out.

He let out a sigh of relief when the next batter hit a pop fly which Craig caught. All the Thoreau fans groaned, while the Sandburg parents let out a cheer that made Tony smile. He was glad for a chance to rest for a few minutes.

But when Tony's team got up to bat, all three batters struck out.

Thoreau was elated. They cheered and shouted, and when Tony walked out to the pitcher's mound at the top of the third, the catcalls were deafening. "We've got you now, Sandburg," their pitcher yelled. "We'll wipe you out!"

"Hold them, Tony!" Craig shouted from third base. Tony could feel the tension even though Sandburg was still two runs ahead.

Jay must have picked up on his nervousness, because he called a time out. "Keep them off-balance," Jay whispered. "Some fastballs, some slow curves. Keep it unpredictable."

Unpredictable. If anyone knew about unpredictable, it was Tony. He thought for a moment of this afternoon, the papers fluttering in the air, his mom shouting, the look on Christy's face when he'd left her.

He bit his lip and wound up. The fastball was straight to the target, but too low. "Ball one!" the umpire called.

A woman was hurrying to the stands, her hair flying in wispy brown strands around her face, her blue coat pulled tightly around her.

How could it be? His mother had been asleep, sound asleep, when he left. His heart seemed to stop. He stared.

The woman waved.

Brent Lewis, on first base, waved back, looking embarrassed. Tony let out a long hissing breath. It was Brent's mother. He could see as she got closer that she was shorter than his mom, and her hair had more red in it.

"Play ball!" the ump shouted impatiently. Tony swallowed. How long had he been standing there like an idiot?

He settled himself on the mound and started his delivery. The pitch was high and outside.

"Ball two!" the ump shouted. Jay signaled for a slow one. Tony knew how to read Jay. He was reminding him to go for control. Tony took a deep breath and nodded. But he could tell as soon as the ball left his hand that it was going to be too low. So was the next one.

"Ball four. Take your base," the ump said.

His control was gone.

THREE STRIKES AND YOU'RE OUT 12

Coach Egan called for a time-out and Tony walked to the baseline. "What's wrong, kid?" he asked. "You were pitching a great game up until now. You want me to put Johnny in?"

Tony shook his head. He'd seen Johnny pitch at practice, and he knew he wasn't ready to pitch in a game yet. Johnny would be scared to death if Coach put him in.

Even if Tony blew it, he'd have to stay on the mound. "It's okay, Coach. I want to stay in."

The coach nodded. "Okay. Go get 'em."

The first two batters grounded out, and to Tony's relief the third batter hit an easy pop fly to third base and ended the inning. But again, Sandburg struck out in the bottom of the third. This game was getting to be a real struggle. Tony tried to keep his focus on the game, but he kept thinking about his mom, and his pitching was uneven. Thoreau was hot now, and in the fourth inning, things really got bad. Thoreau scored three runs, putting them ahead.

Jay talked to Tony between innings, trying to psych him back up. "C'mon, Tony. You can do it. You're the only decent pitcher we've got." Gradually Tony regained some control. In the fifth and sixth innings, even though Thoreau was still getting some hits off of him, Sandburg managed to keep them from scoring.

In the bottom of the sixth, they got a break. Tony and Craig both got on base, and Jay batted them in, to put them one run ahead, before Brent struck out.

"We have to hold them," Jay said to Tony as they conferred on the pitcher's mound before the seventh inning. "This is their last chance. Now's the time for you to burn in some of your ninety-five-mile-an-hour fastballs!"

Tony was feeling wiped, but he managed a grin. "Sure, Jay." His fastball shot across the plate, right on target. Jay gave Tony a thumbs-up, and Tony felt himself starting to loosen up again. He was going to make it. He had his second wind now. His fastball didn't let him down, and he struck out the first two batters. Just a few minutes left to go, and the game would be over. All he had to do was get one more out.

Then it happened.

Thoreau got a hit, and the kid made it to first base. This kid was determined to steal. With every pitch, he lengthened his lead. Jay gestured to Tony, then to Brent at first base. Tony could see Jay was getting rattled. He wanted Tony to try to pick the runner off for the third out. Tony sized up the situation. Brent was out of position, and if Tony's throw went wild, the runner could finish up on third. He might even score.

It was too risky. Tony shook his head and got ready to pitch the ball. He threw a fastball—not ninety-five miles an hour, but a good clean throw. The batter swung and missed.

But Jay, who still had his eyes glued on the runner at first, did something he'd never done before.

He missed the catch.

The ball ricocheted off the backstop and spurted back out toward first base. The runner on first sprinted toward second, then headed for third.

Jay scrambled after the ball, scooped it up, and threw it. Craig Mondale, at third base, bent low for the catch. Tony watched the runner racing toward third. The kid had his head down, paying no attention to the throw coming his way. Tony knew what was going to happen and he winced.

The kid caught the ball right in the gut, and he went down clutching his stomach. The parents in the bleachers gasped, and both coaches ran for the boy.

Tony and the others ran toward him too. Tony stopped when Jay stepped out and grabbed his arm. "He's okay. Just had the wind knocked out of him."

A short man jumped down from the bleachers and ran toward the boy.

"Must be his dad," Jay said, and Tony's eyes suddenly blurred as he watched.

The man bent down and cradled the boy's head against his shoulder. Tony was close enough to hear his anxious question. "You all right, son?"

The boy's eyes opened and he gave his father a dazed grin. "I'm okay, Dad."

Tony remembered then in a sudden flash. He'd been about seven, and had gotten beaned in a neighborhood game. He remembered his dad bending over him, just as this dad was now, and the look of love on his dad's face. Tony looked down at the ground, unable to watch this other boy with the father who cared. He felt a knot forming in his chest.

The boy was standing up now, holding his stomach, and his dad was helping him off the field.

"Play ball," the umpire said. Tony tried. He did his best, but all he could see was the look that the boy and his father had given each other. He felt empty inside. All his energy was gone. After he threw three balls in a row, the coach called another time-out.

He beckoned Tony over to the baseline. Tony walked over to the coach, and stood there, his head down.

"Look, Tony. I'm not blind. Something's bugging you."

"I'm just tired," he mumbled.

The coach put his hands on Tony's shoulders. "I've watched you pitch at practice, Tony. I know what you can do. You've got plenty of energy left, if you just forget whatever's bugging you and focus on the game. The decision is up to you. Do you want to try, or do you want me to put Johnny Scanelli in?"

Tony bit his lip. He knew what he had to do.

He had to concentrate. Forget about everything else, like Coach said, and think about right now. He looked up into Coach's eyes. "I want to stay in."

The coach clapped him on the shoulder. "Good."

He'd done it before. He could do it again. Think about the game—nothing but the game. Tony took a deep breath. Something came together deep inside him, and he felt a surge of energy. He wound up and threw a fastball. He knew by the way it thunked into Jay's mitt that it was a good one.

"Strike one!"

He was back on target.

He threw a slow one. It seemed to hang in the air, and the batter swung too soon.

"Strike two!"

Jay was grinning at him from behind his mask, and Tony felt elation growing inside himself. He could do it. He knew he could do it! But there was no room for error. He had a full count now, three balls and two strikes—and a pinch runner on third, filling in for the kid who'd been hit.

He had to concentrate. The Thoreau team was making catcalls, trying to confuse him, but he focused. All the energy he had inside he willed into his body, into his arm, as he wound up for the pitch.

The ball zipped out of his hand and headed straight and true for the plate.

The batter swung and missed. "Strike three!" the ump called.

It was over. They'd won! With a whoop, the team emptied out on the field and surrounded Tony. He felt himself boosted up on shoulders, and he was getting a lopsided ride back to the dugout. Jay shouted in his ear, "I knew you could do it! What did I tell you, Tony? We're on our way to being city champs!"

Coach Egan was there in the dugout. Tony could see by the look on his face that he was pleased. Jay and Craig set Tony down then and he was surrounded by parents and kids. He grinned as they whacked him on the back, congratulating him. But best was the way he felt inside, a wild joy that he'd never felt before. This was great! From behind him, he heard the coach's voice. "All right, guys. Pile into my van. I'm taking you all over to Pietro's for pizza."

And then, with a thump, Tony came back to reality—his reality.

He had to get home. Christy was alone and maybe scared. His mom was . . . something was wrong with his mom. They were both counting on him. There was no time for pizza parties in his life. He started off the field.

"Hey, Tony! Where you going? The van is over here." It was Jay, hollering at him. Tony didn't look back. He heard heavy footsteps behind him then, and felt a big hand on his shoulder. "Gotta get home?" Coach Egan asked. Tony nodded.

The coach gave his shoulder a squeeze. "Okay. I don't know what's going on, but remember I'm on your side."

Tony couldn't look up at the coach. He was afraid he might start crying. He nodded and kept walking.

Behind him he heard the coach's voice. "By the way, Tony—great game!"

THE CARAMEL SUNDAE   13

Tony pedaled home with the coach's words echoing in his ears.

It was dark now, even though the overhead lights were bright. There were lots of cars going by, but he felt alone. The game—the parents in the bleachers cheering, the kids carrying him on their shoulders—seemed like it had happened a long time ago.

He saw an image in his mind of the kid from the other team and the way his father had looked at him when he'd been hurt. His eyes blurred. He pedaled faster. He had to get home and see how Christy was doing.

The hot fudge sundae. He'd promised her. He backtracked a block to McDonald's and went in. It was crowded with lots of little kids and their parents. The employees all looked tired. He remembered then that the elementary school had had its play tonight; it looked like the whole school had come here afterward. He saw the Bauers and the Jensons on the other side of the room, but he didn't feel like talking to any neighbors. They might ask questions about his mom—or his dad. He got into the farthest line and kept his head down. They were okay neighbors, but they'd never understand what was going on at his house. He didn't understand it himself.

When he finally got to the front of the line, they were out of hot fudge, and he had to get caramel. Christy would be disappointed, but he couldn't help it.

There was a lot of stuff he couldn't help.

He rode home one-handed, carrying the sundae. When he rode into the cul-de-sac he saw that the living room drapes were open and all the lights were on. That was weird. Christy was standing at the window. When he saw the look on her face, he dropped the bike on the lawn and ran for the front door.

"Tony!" Christy ran to him and grabbed his hand, pulling him into the house. She'd been crying and there were dark red splotches on the front of her playsuit.

"Mommy's hurt bad. I tried to talk to her but she won't talk to me and she's bleeding all over."

Blood. That was blood on Christy's playsuit. Tony's heart pounded in his ears, but his voice came out calm. "Where is she, Christy?"

"She's in her room, on the floor. Hurry, Tony."

He suddenly realized he was holding the sundae and set it down on the table. He raced up the stairs behind Christy. "I didn't mean for her to fall, honest, Tony. I couldn't reach the macaroni and cheese, not even with a chair, and I went upstairs and called her and first she was mad and wouldn't come and then she tried to get up out of bed and she fell and she hit"—Christy swallowed—"hit her head on that little table. And she's bleeding bad."

She was on the floor, just inside the bedroom door, and she wasn't moving. There was a lot of blood. He felt dizzy, like he might faint, but he couldn't. There was no one here but him to do something.

911. The emergency number. He grabbed the phone off the table beside the bed and dialed. A calm voice on the other end answered almost immediately.

"My mom's hurt. I think we need an ambulance," he heard himself saying. There was a roaring sound in his ears. He sat down on the bed. The woman's voice asked questions: Address? Main intersection by house? He answered her numbly, then hung up. He thought he heard the voice say something just as he put the phone down. Maybe he was supposed to stay on the line.

But he had to do something about the blood. He went into the bathroom and grabbed a towel and washcloth. Christy followed him, not saying anything, her face white. He wet the cloth, then went back in and knelt down beside his mother. He wiped the blood off her forehead. More blood gushed out. Tony felt sick. He pressed the towel over the bloody spot and his mom moaned. He pulled back. He took deep breaths to calm down.

At least she was alive.

He heard the sirens then. So soon. How did they get here so fast? People always said they took a long time. He went down the stairs to open the door. Christy followed, hanging on to his hand. It was two paramedics. They were carrying black bags, just like in the movies, Tony thought. The older man reminded Tony of Uncle Jeff. He asked Tony quick questions, but he was kind. Then the two men hurried up the stairs. They bent over his mother, checking her and murmuring to each other in quiet voices. Tony sat down on the side of the bed. He felt weak with his sudden relief. These two knew what they were doing. He didn't have to do anything now. Christy huddled up against him.

Then he saw the bottle, next to the pitcher of orange juice by the bed. It was almost empty. But it had been half-full when he looked in before the game. Could she have drunk all that?

One of the paramedics, the young one, stood up and looked around. He saw the bottle right away, it seemed. Almost as if he were searching for it. He walked over and picked it up. He looked at the other paramedic, and Tony saw the look they exchanged.

The younger paramedic knelt down by Christy. "You look scared, honey. It's okay. I don't think your mom is hurt that bad."

"She's bleeding so much," Christy whispered.

"I know. It looks like she hit her head on the corner of this table when she fell. Scalp wounds bleed a lot. But they're not usually serious. We'll bandage it up."

"Are you going to take her to the hospital?" Christy asked.

He nodded. "We have to check her, just to make

sure nothing else is wrong." He looked at Tony. "Do you know where your dad is, or a relative you can stay with for a little while?"

What should he say? His throat was dry, and his tongue felt thick in his mouth when he spoke. "My . . . my dad's on a business trip. He's been moving around a lot. I don't know where he is now."

"I do," Christy said. Tony watched, stunned, as she walked over to the other side of the bed, tugged open the bottom drawer of his mother's dresser, and pulled out a handful of letters shoved into the corner.

"Those are old letters, Christy," he said.

She shook her head. "Uh-uh. I saw Mommy put one here yesterday." She looked scared then; she clamped her hand over her mouth and looked down at Mom lying on the floor. But she was still unconscious.

The paramedic looked at the return address on the letter and frowned. "California, huh? Maybe we can get a phone number from information."

"Do you have any relatives in the area?" the older paramedic asked.

Tony shook his head. Christy tugged on his arm. "Tony, we have Uncle Jeff. Mommy wrote down his number for me this morning, remember? I called him all by myself." She took a crumpled piece of paper from her pocket and handed it to the paramedic. He took it from her and dialed. He waited for several moments. "No answer," he said. "What about a neighbor?"

Tony hesitated. His stomach was feeling bad now, and he swallowed a couple of times before he answered. "The Lyndens are on vacation and most of our other neighbors went to a school play. We'll be okay by ourselves. I take care of Christy a lot of the time."

The two paramedics exchanged glances again.

"We'd better take you with us. We'll try to get hold of your uncle when we get to the hospital."

The next few minutes were a blur. The paramedics took Mom out on a stretcher. She was moaning but she still didn't open her eyes. Tony felt detached from her, as if she were someone in a movie he was watching.

The paramedic left a note and a number on the front table, "just in case someone comes in while we're gone." This struck Tony funny—who would come in while they were gone? A burglar, maybe?

He obediently followed the paramedics downstairs, Christy still holding tightly to his hand. But on the way out he saw the sundae, sitting on the table where he'd left it. The lid had popped open and a sticky brown puddle of caramel had leaked out on the table. His stomach lurched. He pulled his hand away from Christy, ran into the front bathroom, and threw up.

THE HOSPITAL WAITING ROOM 14

The paramedics waited for him by the front door. "Don't feel bad. That happens a lot," the older one said. They went out to the ambulance and the older paramedic gave Tony a barf bag to hold on the trip to the hospital. But he didn't need it anymore. His stomach was just an empty ache now. Christy was quiet. She held on to Tony's arm and looked out the window. Once she looked at him and said, "I didn't know what to do when Mommy fell. I asked the Nanakins, but they didn't know either."

The driver didn't seem to be paying attention. Tony was glad. He didn't feel like explaining about the Nanakins.

"How come the siren's not on?" Christy asked.

The driver answered. "No traffic tonight, honey.

We don't need it for the few miles we have to go. Besides, your mom is going to be okay. I know it looks scary, but we didn't find anything serious when we checked her at the house."

Nothing serious. Tony felt like laughing again. The driver should live at their house awhile. But then again, whatever was wrong with his mom didn't seem to show on the outside. At least not to most people.

The ambulance pulled into the emergency hospital entrance and the driver jumped out. "You two come in with me. I'll introduce you to Marla and she'll try to call your uncle Jeff again." He opened the door on their side and helped Christy out. Tony followed. The driver was talking to a lady at the desk—Marla, he guessed. She nodded and came over to them. "Now, kids. Don't worry. Everything is going to be all right." She hovered, speaking reassuring words that didn't mean a thing. Tony tuned out.

He felt tired. He just wanted to sit down and fall asleep. Then he saw his mom. They were wheeling her in on one of those gurney things, and her eyes were closed.

His heart squeezed, when he looked at her. She was so pale, and she had that big bandage over her forehead. Her hair was matted, sticking out in all directions. It was the blood that made it stick together that way. He looked away.

The lady from the desk was still talking. He realized she was trying to get them to go into the other room. She had one hand on his arm, and her other arm around Christy's shoulder. "Come on, kids. You can wait in here for your uncle Jeff. There's a TV and some magazines. Are you hungry? I could call Dietary and have them send something down. A sandwich, maybe, or some Jell-O?"

The thought of food made Tony sick. He didn't answer. Christy said, "Do you have red Jell-O? The Nana—I like red Jell-O."

"Sure, honey. You go ahead and see if there's something good on TV and I'll get the Jell-O. Maybe your brother can check the channels for you. Just push that button to change them." She walked briskly back to her receptionist's desk. Tony saw her on the phone.

It was quiet in the waiting area. They were the only ones there. There was one light on, over in the corner, and it shed a narrow circle of light on a pile of old magazines.

"Tony, do you think Mommy is going to die?"

Christy's face was smudged with tears, and a couple of brown streaks—dried blood, he realized with a jolt. From Mom. He saw a stack of napkins by the coffee machine. He wet one at the drinking fountain and wiped off Christy's face.

"She's not going to die. You heard what the paramedics said. She's not hurt bad."

"What if he's not telling the truth, Tony? Sometimes grown-ups lie."

Yeah, Tony thought. Tell me about it. But to Christy he said, "He's telling the truth. Do you want to watch TV now? This looks like an old Shirley Temple movie."

"Tony, why didn't the Nanakins tell me what to do when Mommy fell?"

He felt anger stirring inside him. "The Nanakins are just pretend. They can't tell you stuff like that. You have to decide for yourself."

"But they told me about the dog that was chasing you."

Tony sighed. "That was you, Christy. I don't know exactly how to explain it, but you really like animals, and somehow you knew, inside, that dog just wanted to play."

Christy folded her arms. "I don't care what you

say. The Nanakins are still my friends. Even if they didn't tell me what to do about Mommy. They always listen to me, and they never get mad."

Tony didn't say anything.

"Turn to Shirley Temple now, Tony. I like that one. That's when she sings 'Animal Crackers in My Soup.'"

Marla was walking back toward them, a smile on her face. Why did people smile when things were the worst? "I got your uncle Jeff. He's on his way over. He sounds nice."

"He is nice," Christy said. "Uncle Jeff and me even talk about the Nanakins." She looked worried then, and Tony knew she was wishing she hadn't mentioned them to Marla. It didn't make any difference though. Marla didn't ask any questions. "Here's your Jell-O, honey." She handed a plastic bowl of red Jell-O to Christy, along with a little plastic spoon. "Are you sure you don't want anything, Tony?" He shook his head, and Marla bustled back to her desk.

Christy ate Jell-O and watched Shirley Temple while Tony stared off into space. He wondered what they were doing to his mom right now. Probably cleaning up the cut on her head. He'd had stitches in his lip once, when he was seven, and it had really hurt. He remembered how scared he'd been and his mom had held him tight. He remembered her saying, "It's okay, honey. It's okay."

It had been okay—then.

He swallowed. Why couldn't he get rid of this lump in his throat? And why the heck wasn't his dad here while all this was happening? Why was Tony always the one who had to take care of things?

He leaned his head back against the brown vinyl of the chair. He was starting to get a headache. Nothing made sense anymore. He was scared, and the roller coaster kept plunging down one curve after another.

The hospital doors slid open and Tony looked up.

It was Uncle Jeff. He'd grown a beard since Tony had seen him last, and it took a minute before Tony realized who it was. But when he smiled, there was no mistaking him. "Christy! Tony!" Uncle Jeff started toward them.

Christy jumped down and ran into his arms. Tony stood there, watching them, wishing he could run into Uncle Jeff's arms too, and make it all better. But he couldn't. All he could think about now was his mother unconscious on the stretcher, that bleeding gash on her head.

The Blowup **15**

On the way to Uncle Jeff's house, Tony stared out the side window of the car. It was so dark. Uncle Jeff lived in an older part of town and there were hardly any streetlights.

"I talked to your dad about an hour ago," Uncle Jeff said. "He's trying to get a flight back here tonight. He'll call as soon as he knows."

Tony straightened up. "How did you know where to call him?"

Uncle Jeff was quiet for a few moments and then he said, "Your dad's called several times the last couple of weeks, Tony. He's been worried. He said he's tried to call home, but no one answers."

Christy was curled up in a ball beside Tony. She looked up at him. "Mommy kept the answering machine on," she said. "I asked her how come she erased the messages, but she said it was just people selling stuff. She wouldn't let me answer the phone."

His dad *had* tried to call. Tony sat there, thinking. Well, so what? If he really cared he wouldn't have gone away at all. It was all his dad's fault that this had happened. His mom couldn't take care of everything by herself, and neither could Tony.

They were at Uncle Jeff's now and Aunt Karen met them at the door. "Your dad called a few minutes ago," she said to Tony and Christy. "He's got a flight out late tonight, and he'll be in early in the morning. He's leaving for the airport now."

Christy squealed. "Daddy's coming home. Yea!"

Tony stood there, not saying anything. Aunt Karen came over to him and put an arm around his shoulder. "You must be tired. Come on, honey. I'll put some sheets on the bed for you."

Aunt Karen led him into a blue-and-white bedroom. He knew he wouldn't be able to sleep. He felt mad, really mad at his dad. *Now* he was coming back. Now was too late. Everything was too screwed up. He thought of his mom with the gash on her head. He thought of the vodka bottle beside the bed, and the bottles in the trash. Quickly he pushed that memory out of his mind.

He sat down on the bed, and the tiredness took over again. He just couldn't think anymore. None of it made sense. He vaguely sensed Aunt Karen helping him with his shoes, and then everything seemed blurry and far away.

The next thing he knew he was awake, and it was morning. He lay there, surprised that he had slept all night. He hadn't even dreamed. He heard footsteps and a knock, then Uncle Jeff pushed the door open and looked in. "You awake, sport? Your dad's here. He's downstairs having breakfast, and he wants to see you."

Tony got out of bed. He still felt tired, as tired as if he hadn't slept at all. His bones felt heavy, and he had to drag himself around as he got dressed.

When he got to the kitchen, Christy was already there, her arms wrapped around her father's neck.

Tony stood in the doorway, not knowing what to say. His father looked thinner than he had when he'd left, smaller somehow. And he looked older too.

"I've missed you, Tony," he said. He set Christy down and stood up.

"Then why did you stay away?" Tony asked. The anger flooded back, filling him.

"I'm sorry I did that. We'll talk about it later." His dad held out his arms, but Tony stood there stiffly. His dad sighed. He walked over and gave Tony's shoulder a squeeze. "Why don't you get some breakfast, and then we'll go home."

Tony was silent on the drive home. He was worried about Mom, but he was so angry at his dad, he didn't want to ask about her. He figured his dad would say something if things were any worse. Christy made up for his silence. She chattered all the way, filling Dad in on everything she'd done since he'd left. Tony stared out the window, trying to hold in the fury that filled every part of him. When they pulled into the driveway, Christy jumped out. "Hurry, Daddy, unlock the door. I don't want to miss 'Sesame Street.' " She ran into the family room. In a moment, Tony heard the sounds of Big Bird and Oscar coming from the set.

He stood with his dad in the front hall, neither of them speaking for a moment. His dad looked awkward, standing there with his hands in his pockets. "Are you worried about Mom?" he asked finally.

"Yes," Tony said.

"I saw her early this morning. The cut was just a scalp wound. She doesn't have a concussion, but the doctor wants to do a few more tests before she comes home." Something about his father's tone of voice made Tony suspicious. "What do you mean, some more tests?"

"Tony," his dad said, "let's go out on the deck for a few minutes. I need to talk to you."

Tony's throat clenched closed again. So his mom really was sick. It must be something bad. His anger faded away with this new fear. He followed his father through the living room and out onto the deck. He sat down on the porch swing and waited. His father stood looking down at him. "Tony," he said, "there *is* something wrong with Mom."

His dad paused, as if to gather courage. "She . . . your mom is an alcoholic."

The words hung there, not making any sense to Tony, as if he'd suddenly found himself in some foreign country, unable to communicate with the people there.

An alcoholic? Alcoholics were the people down on First Avenue. The ones that shuffled around in the middle of the morning with wine bottles inside brown paper bags, sleeping on the benches at night. He'd seen them when he'd been downtown with his mom shopping. His mom wasn't like that.

"Tony, do you understand what I'm trying to tell you?" his father asked. "The doctor's going to try to talk to Mom, to see if she'll go into an alcohol treatment center."

Tony stared at his father, rage building inside him. "*No!*" he shouted. "You're the one who needs treatment. Something's wrong with *you*! *You're* the one who went off to build your stupid business. It's your fault Mom's sick. So she had a few drinks while you were gone! That doesn't mean she's an alcoholic. It's because you left her alone!"

He was shaking, shaking all over, even on the inside. His father reached out toward him, but Tony pulled back.

"Tony, she's been drinking for a long time. That's why I left. I didn't know how to deal with it. I thought if I got away for a little while, maybe I'd figure out what to do."

Tony clenched his fists to stop the shaking. He could feel his nails digging into his palms. His dad kept talking. "I shouldn't have left you and Christy here alone with your mom. I'm sorry. But I'm back now, and I've found out some ways to help. There's help for Mom when she's ready for it—and for you and me and Christy."

Tony stared at him, not believing what he was hearing. "I don't need any help!" he shouted. "I just need you out of my life!"

He turned and ran down the back steps.

ANOTHER TRIP TO THE HOSPITAL

16

The shed door was standing open. Tony jerked on the handlebars of his bike, trying to pull it out. It was tangled with Christy's small one and wouldn't budge. His dad started down the stairs. "Calm down, Tony. Remember, I love your mom too."

"Liar!" Tony shouted. He saw Christy standing on the deck watching him, her eyes wide.

His dad was beside him. He reached out to put a hand on Tony's shoulder. Tony pulled away. "You hate her!" he yelled. "That's why you left. That's why all this happened. It's all your fault!" He jerked at the bike again and knocked a plastic box of screws off the shelf above. It fell to the floor and popped open, the screws rolling in every direction.

He yanked again, furiously, and the bike pulled loose from the tangle. He was breathing hard as he backed it out of the shed. "Tony, wait," his dad said.

Tony kept going. He wheeled his bike to the side of the house and got on. He tore out into the street, pedaling furiously, seeing only a blur of houses and cars. He turned onto Jefferson. He jumped his bike up onto the curb and kept going. His wheel caught suddenly in the groove, and he pitched forward off the bike, and landed in the street. There was the squeal of brakes, and a white-faced man jumped out of his car.

"You okay, kid?"

"Yeah, sure." His face felt wet. Instinctively he wiped it on the corner of his shirt, staring at the wetness. It couldn't be tears. He wasn't crying. He knew he wasn't crying. He jumped back on the bike.

"Hey, wait a minute!" the guy called. But Tony kept going. He rode more carefully now, on the sidewalk instead of the curb. His heart kept pounding. His mind spun pictures faster than he could think of them. His mom. He'd go see his mom. She'd tell him the truth. She'd tell him that his dad was a liar, that she wasn't an alcoholic. She'd explain about the bottles. There'd be a reason, he knew it.

Would they let him in at the hospital? Why not—he was her son. He was only a few blocks from the park-and-ride. One of the buses must go to Interlake Hospital. He rode deliberately now—fast, but watching where he was going. A bus was just pulling into the park-and-ride. He locked his bike up hastily and ran to where the bus was waiting, doors open. The sign on the front said number 220.

Two old ladies carrying umbrellas got off. The bus driver looked bored, sitting there, staring off into space. "What bus do I take to get to Interlake Hospital?" Tony asked.

The driver looked down at him. "You can get there on this one." Tony fished around in his pocket and pulled out some change. He had enough to get there and back, just barely. The bus was empty, except for a college kid reading a paperback novel and an older man who was doing a crossword puzzle. Neither one looked up when Tony got on the bus.

He sat down in the back and stared out the window. He tried to look at the view, to make his mind go blank. He forced himself to take deep breaths. He thought about the game last night. Baseball was the one good thing in his life right now. And even that—how could he keep playing? If he hadn't gone to the game, his mom wouldn't have gotten hurt. That was his fault.

He should have known enough to get dinner for Christy before he left, or at least to get something down for her. He'd blown it again.

"Hey, kid," the bus driver called back. "You transfer here. Take the number seven. It'll let you off right in front of the hospital. It's only about a mile from here."

Tony got off. Within a few minutes the number seven pulled up, and a few minutes later he saw Interlake Hospital in front of him. He got off and stared up at the huge white building. There were hundreds of windows. Was his mom looking out one of them?

Don't be stupid, he said to himself. She's probably asleep. He took a deep breath and walked in. There were rest rooms right inside, and he decided he better clean up a little.

He was shocked when he looked in the mirror. His eyes looked like two holes in his face, and his left cheek was scratched and streaked with dirt from the fall. He washed his face, and smoothed his hair down the best he could with his fingers.

He took a couple of deep breaths and went back out to the information desk. The lady there didn't seem shocked or anything, so he guessed he looked okay. She directed him to the fifth floor. "Check with the desk clerk there," she said. "It looks like her room was changed during the night, but she's still on the same floor."

He took the elevator. His stomach dropped. He didn't know if it was because of the sudden jolt when the elevator stopped, or because he was so scared. The nurse at the desk frowned when he asked for Eileen Peterson's room. "I'm her son," he said.

She stared at him over the top of her glasses. "Sit down here," she said. "I'll see if she can have visitors."

They weren't going to let him in. Tony could feel it. They knew something was wrong. He could tell from the looks on their faces. He fidgeted on the hard chair. Maybe he could sneak in. He had to see her. But he didn't know which room was hers, and besides, the other nurse at the desk was watching him.

It seemed forever before the first nurse returned,

her shoes making little hissing sounds against the floor. But it was only eight minutes, according to the big clock over the nurse's desk.

"Come with me, Tony," she said, and her voice was almost pleasant. "You can see your mom for a few minutes. She's had some medication, so she may be sleepy."

He thought he was prepared, but he still felt his legs go weak when he walked in and saw her lying on the bed. She looked small under the blankets, and her face was still pale. She had a bandage that covered all of her forehead, as well as the top of her head. But the blood was gone. "Mom," he whispered, and his throat felt dry, so dry the words hardly came out. Her eyes fluttered open for a moment and she smiled.

"Tony." She opened her hand and he walked over to her and put his hand in hers. She squeezed it just a little.

"You okay, honey?" she asked sleepily. He bit his lip, not daring to say anything for a minute.

He swallowed, and took in a deep breath. "You scared us when you fell."

"Sorry, honey." She opened her eyes again and looked at him. "It's okay, Tony. Don't look so scared. Give me a hug." She smiled faintly. "But be gentle. I've got a few sore spots."

He bent over and brushed his cheek against hers. Then he stood watching her. "Mom, what's wrong? Why did you fall?"

She frowned slightly, as if trying to remember something. Her face smoothed out then, and she looked up at him. "Just a little relapse from that flu, honey. I got dizzy. It's nothing to worry about."

"Dad said . . ." The words popped out, and then he swallowed the rest down.

She opened her eyes then and looked at him, and he saw that hardness again. "Dad said what?"

He looked at her. "Nothing." He couldn't do it. He couldn't say it. It wasn't true anyway.

She was sick, and he shouldn't make it worse by saying something that would upset her. He stood there silently. Neither one of them said anything about Dad being back, after all this time. It was like they were both pretending that this was expected.

She patted his hand. "Your father's upset because I fell and got hurt, honey. You know how he overreacts. I'll be fine. . . ." Her voice faded again and she closed her eyes.

The nurse was standing in the doorway. "You'll

have to leave now, Tony. If you want to come back
with your dad this evening, you can."

He followed her obediently down the hallway.
"How are you getting home?" the nurse asked.
"Your dad said to call if you need a ride."

So they'd called his dad.

"I don't need a ride," he said. "I took the bus."

The nurse looked uncertain. "Thanks for letting
me go in," Tony said. He hurried onto the elevator
and pressed the button before the nurse could stop
him.

Outside, a bus was at the curb waiting and Tony
got on. He felt suspended in space. It didn't seem
to matter where the bus was going.

In just a few minutes, though, he saw the transfer stop, and got off. He had to wait for a 220 to
take him back to where his bike was. It seemed as
though he waited forever. He tried to think just
about baseball. He'd pitched such a great last inning
last night. The other boys acted like he was a hero.
So much had happened since then, it felt like the
game had been weeks ago instead of just last night.

Finally the 220 came. He sat in the back and
stared out at the traffic as the bus rocked along.

When he got off, he unlocked his bike and rode
home. When he passed the clock at the drugstore,

it was only 4:30. He'd been gone less than three hours.

When Tony rode into the cul-de-sac, his dad was looking out the front window. He dropped the curtain quickly, as if he didn't want Tony to catch him looking out.

Well, so what? His dad didn't really care about him. He'd just yell at him for running off.

But when he walked in the back door, his dad hesitantly put a hand on his shoulder and said, "Tony?"

Tony brushed by him and went upstairs to his room.

JUST PRETENDING   **17**

He waited, half expecting his dad to come up after him, but he didn't. Tony dozed off. When he woke up, he realized he was hungry. He hadn't eaten since breakfast, and not much then. He got up and went slowly down the stairs. Something smelled good. He found himself drawn, almost against his will, to the kitchen. His dad and Christy were sitting at the table, eating plates of something unfamiliar that smelled good.

Christy grinned at him. "It's fetta . . . fetta . . ."

"Fettuccine," their dad finished. "Pull up a chair and have some, Tony. It's my new specialty."

"It's supergood, Tony," Christy said. "It's got lots of that kind of white cheese that you like."

"Mozzarella," her dad said.

Tony hesitated. He didn't want to be here with his father, but he felt like he'd get sick if he didn't eat something soon. He got a plate out of the cupboard and sat down.

"We already said a blessing," Christy said. "So don't worry, Tony. I blessed you too." She wound a huge mouthful of fettuccine on her fork and shoved it into her mouth. Tony concentrated on the food. He filled his plate with fettuccine and ate without looking up.

Christy was telling their father about the Dad's Night coming up at school and what he should wear to it.

Tony took a quick look at Christy. She looked happy, talking to Dad. Did she remember that he had deserted her for six months?

Tony finished the fettuccine, took his plate to the sink, rinsed it, and put it in the dishwasher. Then he went back up to his room.

For the next three days, Tony avoided his father as much as possible. His dad didn't question him. He called Tony to meals and each day he asked if Tony wanted to go to see his mom.

Tony didn't.

He couldn't put his fears into words, but just

the thought of being in the hospital room again made him feel cold all over. He spent his time in his bedroom—when he wasn't at school, doing his route, or at baseball practice.

At school he was a hero. Jay and Craig treated him like royalty, telling all the kids how Tony had saved the game against Thoreau. At school and at baseball practice, Tony felt almost happy. He could put everything else out of his mind then—almost. He didn't need to rush home anymore afterward. Christy was taken care of now. Tony knew he'd find her having a good dinner and talking to Dad when he got home. He didn't need to clean the kitchen anymore, or do the laundry either. His dad was taking care of all that now.

But that didn't ease Tony's anger. His dad could never do anything to make up for the six months away. And whatever was wrong with his mom was all his dad's fault.

Mostly, he tried not to think about that. But sometimes thoughts would pop into his mind, when he was riding his bike, or when he was in bed at night. Little disjointed thoughts about the orange juice his mom drank, and those bottles he'd found in the trash.

He found a bunch of stuff in the bathroom magazine basket, brochures about alcoholism. His dad had put them there, he knew, which made him determined not to read any of them. But he found himself reading little snatches. It reminded him of stuff he'd heard at school when they talked about drug and alcohol abuse—stuff he'd tried to forget. The sick feeling in his stomach told him that some of this made sense. It explained how his mom was acting.

He threw the brochures back in the basket. It wasn't possible. This couldn't all be happening. She'd be home any day now, and she'd be fine. He tried not to think beyond that.

On Friday, just as he was coming in from his paper route, he heard his dad on the kitchen phone. He stood in the hall and listened.

"It's taken several days just to detoxify her," his dad was saying. "She must have been drinking steadily for that last week . . . or more. Then, when the real estate deal fell through, it was too much for her."

Tony's pulse roared in his ears, but he stayed where he was, as if glued to the spot.

His dad was listening on the phone, and when he spoke again, his voice sounded sad. "No, Jeff. She doesn't want to admit it. She says she just had a few drinks to help her shake the flu. She's in total denial."

He listened and sighed again. "I don't know. She'll be coming home Tuesday, I guess. There's nothing else they can do, if she doesn't want to go into treatment."

Tony tried to control his ragged breathing. His dad was just ending the phone conversation. "I'll tell you one thing, Jeff. This time I'll be here. I won't leave these kids again. That was the biggest mistake I made."

He hung up then. Tony hurried down the hall the other way and up the stairs. Christy was sitting on her bed with a pile of ribbons in front of her. She looked up as he went by her room. "Tony," she asked, "which ribbon should I wear? Daddy and me are going to your game tonight."

Tony looked at her. He didn't want his father to go to his game, but what could he say? He couldn't stop him, and besides, he knew how much Christy wanted to go. He walked over and picked up a purple ribbon. "This one," he said.

Christy grinned. "That's the one the Nanakins said too."

Tony sighed. "Christy, the Nanakins are just pretend; don't you know that yet?"

114

Christy nodded. "I know. Daddy and me been talking about the Nanakins. And he says pretend is okay, as long as I don't get it mixed up with real." She looked reproachfully at Tony. "And I think you should stop being so mean to Daddy."

Tony walked out of the room.

SAFE AT HOME   18

When Tony walked out to the pitcher's mound that night, his hands felt sweaty. He wiped them on his pants and threw his first pitch. It was a fastball and it zipped across the plate right where he'd pictured it.

"Strike one!" the ump hollered.

Tony looked up into the stands and saw his dad and Christy, smiling and cheering for him. All of a sudden his heart felt as if it were too big to fit in his chest.

The game was a tough one, and by the seventh inning, Tony was tired. The score was tied 2–2 when he went up to bat. On the first pitch he got a hit, a good one. He thought when he heard the crack of the bat that it was a homer, but he couldn't be sure.

He ran, not looking back, hearing the familiar chant in his ears as he rounded third and headed for home.

"Slide, Tony, slide!"

He could hear the coach's voice and Jay's, and then Christy's high-pitched shriek, and his dad's deep voice.

"*Slide!*"

He did, and heard the umpire's welcome shout, as he lay there, trying to catch his breath.

"Safe at home!"

He looked up into the stands in spite of himself and saw his dad's big grin. And then Christy shouted, "That's my brother!" and everybody laughed.

Afterward, when Sandburg had won the game, the crowd in the bleachers poured out onto the field. There was lots of hugging and screaming, and the boys pounded one another on the shoulders. Tony hardly realized he'd hugged his dad in all the confusion. His dad looked really happy and Tony felt a strange feeling inside. He wanted to hug him again. But then he thought about his mother and how it was all his dad's fault, and he pulled away.

The coach said, "Everyone to Pietro's for pizza," and some of the guys went in the car with Tony and Christy and his dad. They laughed and ate pizza and Tony felt himself unwinding and letting go. Jay poured orange pop on his shoulder, and Tony sneaked a piece of pizza into Jay's pocket so that Jay got a handful of cheese and pepperoni when he reached in for some quarters for the video game. For a little while, Tony felt like a kid, like he didn't have a worry in the world. It felt good.

But it only lasted for a little while and then they were home, and the gray feeling came back.

His mom would be back on Tuesday. What would happen then?

He walked aimlessly around the house Monday afternoon after school. Christy was sitting on the living room floor playing with her paper dolls, and she looked upset.

"Tony, are you mad at me?"

Tony stopped. "Mad at you for what?"

"Because I made Mommy fall, and then Daddy came home. And you hate Daddy."

Tony felt like the breath was knocked out of him. He sat down beside her. "Christy, it's not your fault Mom fell. Sometimes things just happen."

"Then how come you hate Daddy? Do you think it's his fault."

Yes! Tony wanted to shout. Yes! But he realized

how stupid that was. Blaming his dad was just as stupid as Christy blaming herself. Tony couldn't say anything. Something big was welling up inside him, something he wanted to hold back down and not let out.

"Tony, Daddy's being so nice. Aren't you glad he's here to take care of us now? I am."

"Christy, he'll just leave again, when Mom gets better. Don't you know that?" Tony said.

"He will not," Christy said. "He asked his boss to not make him work in those other places anymore, and now he'll be here, and he won't make so much money, but he doesn't care because he can take care of us, and Mommy too."

"If he took care of Mom before, she wouldn't have gotten sick," Tony said.

Christy looked at him. "Mommy's an alc . . . alcoholic, Tony. And that's a sickness. And Daddy's going to take me to a special meeting with him tonight to talk about it. And they have cookies there. It's called Ala-something. The Nanakins are going too."

She grinned at Tony. "But it's okay, because I know the Nanakins are just pretend. But I still like to play them, and sometimes Daddy and me play them together."

Tony started to walk out of the room, but Christy's voice followed him. "Daddy says he was pretending too, when he went away. But he told me that was a bad kind of pretending, because he got it mixed up with real. He was pretending that everything would be all right. And when he was away he pretended we were just fine and he's sorry he did that."

Tony turned the corner, willing himself to stop listening. But one thought kept nagging at him.

Was he pretending too?

He walked into the kitchen. His dad was taking some cookies out of the oven. Tony started to back out, but it was too late. His dad looked up and smiled. "Have a cookie," he said. "They're burned on the bottom, but not too bad."

Tony shook his head but he sat down at the table anyway. His dad looked at him. "Tony, I know you're mad at me. And you have every right to be. I really screwed up, and I deserted you. I didn't think that's what I was doing but that's what I did."

Tony bit his lip and didn't say anything.

His dad's voice was serious. "I won't leave you again, I promise. From now on we're in this together."

Tony just sat there for a minute, but he could feel the words rising slowly inside him, as if they had to come out, finally. "What are we going to do about Mom?" His voice sounded hoarse but he kept on going. "When she comes home tomorrow, are you going to tell her she's . . . an alcoholic?" His throat stuck on the word and he almost whispered it. But as soon as he said it, he knew it was true. Mom's drinking wasn't his dad's fault, no matter how much he wanted to believe it.

She was an alcoholic.

His dad was silent for a moment. "I don't know what I'll say, Tony. She already knows what I think. She's not ready to hear it yet." His dad reached across the table and put his hand on Tony's shoulder. "We'll do the best we can."

He looked into Tony's eyes. "One more promise: You don't have to run the house anymore. I'm here to see that you get to have some time with your friends."

Should he trust him? Tony could feel the struggle going on inside himself, and then . . .

It was almost like something melting inside. It was the opposite of what he usually did, of the tight concentration he forced himself to have so often.

121

The heavy knot that seemed to have been in his stomach forever started to ease.

It felt good.

At least he could give his dad a chance. He could stop pretending that it was all his dad's fault. He wasn't sure how it would work, but he could try. And now, with his dad here, he could play baseball.

Baseball. He thought about the game last night, and how he'd felt when he made the home run, and the look on his dad's face.

And he remembered the ump's voice ringing out when he slid into home plate.

"Safe!" Safe at home!

Tony looked up from the table. His dad was watching him. He stood up and came around to Tony's side of the table.

For a minute he just stood there, the two of them looking at each other. Then his dad bent down and his arms were around him.

Tony hugged him back. He was surprised how good it felt. He felt safe with his dad's arms around him. Safe at home, he thought. And he smiled a secret grin.

Maybe it was really true.